WRECKED

"After reading *Wrecked*, I am the title. Ate it up
in one gulp because I couldn't look away.
Tragic, compelling, real, and beautifully written."
Teri Terry

www.guppybooks.co.uk

WRECKED

LOUISA REID

GUPPY BOOKS

WRECKED
is a GUPPY BOOK

First published in 2020 by
Guppy Publishing Ltd,
Bracken Hill,
Cotswold Road,
Oxford OX2 9JG

Text © Louisa Reid, 2020

978 1 913101 36 7

1 3 5 7 9 10 8 6 4 2

Papers used by Guppy Books are from well-managed forests and other responsible sources.

GUPPY PUBLISHING LTD Reg. No. 11565833

A CIP catalogue record for this book is available from the British Library.

Typeset in Gill Sans by Falcon Oast Graphic Art Ltd, www.falcon.uk.com
Printed and bound in Great Britain by CPI Books Ltd

> *"You said a bad driver was only safe until she met another bad driver? Well, I met another bad driver, didn't I?"*
>
> *The Great Gatsby*, F Scott Fitzgerald

PART ONE

NOW

BOXED

Court room,

Caught room.   I'm in the dock.

There's no way out.

All exits blocked.

ALL RISE

Jury,
then judge.

There's a hush.

I want to burst it,
take a pin to its weight,
explode the silence –

escape.

Head down,
arms out,
I'll speed through these walls,
like I'm made of steel –
like I can't fall.

I'll
        spread my   wings wide,
                taste air,   breathe
                                sky.

But facts are – I'm trapped –
stiff shirt like a noose,
new suit, buttoned up;
strait-jacketed truth.

CHARGES

"Joseph Goodenough.

In the early hours of
The first
Of January
Two thousand and nineteen,

You are accused of causing the
Death
Of **Stephanie White**.

To the charge of
Death
By **Dangerous Driving**.

How do you plead?''

STOP

I'm winded,
almost doubled over –

That's all it takes to put me
there – again,
in that black, dark night,
on that black, dark road,
with Imogen, just Imogen,
by my side.

And I shut my eyes
to hide from the scene,

but

there's light

coming at us

from around a dark corner

it's tunnelling forwards

it's upon us,

almost,

it's

bright,

it's

full beam

it's

up

in our faces –

and

we're driving

straight

at

it

can't stop –

are we braking?

But

there's no

way

out

because

these seconds are small,

and this car is so huge,

and the wheel won't turn

it's heavy and slow

we're out of control

it's still coming at us

so fast,

horn blaring

lights flashing

Jesus,

please

STOP —

IMOGEN —

NO.

DEAD

Not Imogen, not me,
but
the woman in the other car.

I staggered up the road
towards the wreck
and saw

               a body,

                    (or something like)

and a jagged   hole
where the side of the car   should have been.

I stared at
white bones.

Saw
red skin stretched

into a silent scream.

Torso twisted,
face glassed
into

8

```
p            e            e
        i            c            s
```

I howled.

She didn't twitch.

Her blonde hair in a plait.
Scalped.

Finished.

DAWN

When I'm lying in bed
crawling up, out of whatever sleep
I've caught that night
it's almost not there,
I've almost forgotten to remember,
and then
before I can open my eyes on the day
that dead body slaps me awake.

She's always wearing white,

her blood pulses and glows
dripping, staining, seeping
over her clothes.

And I'm running to the bathroom
throwing up in the sink
spewing nothing –
empty belly
twisting with
guilt.

WHAT DO YOU PLEAD?

They're waiting.

Why can't I say it?
I need to respond,
and I open my mouth like I practised this morning
in front of the mirror, in front of my mum.

Not guilty, I said then,
pulling the words up and out from inside,
like fish

flapping and flailing,

                    caught on a line.

I try once again –
open my mouth, and breathe

but   the   sounds are stuck
in   my   t h r o a t
I can't   squeeze   them   free,

"N-"
the first sound comes
and then the rest in a rush,
"Not guilty," I say
convincing no one,
not even myself.

Because I'm still at the scene –
stuck
in the past, in the frame,
here in the dock,
frozen with shame.

TRUTH (i)

It shouldn't be this hard to tell the truth –
to   spit   it   right   out,
(like the teachers used to tell me,
when I couldn't make a sound).

Small Joe stuttered and big Joe's no better,
not now he's trying to makes sense of the senseless.

Because – and don't ask me why – the truth is
elusive, it swerves and it slides –
like the car did that night –

                                        now it's greasy with lies.

The truth is shattered, like the glass on the road
that I find in my hair, in my dreams and
my clothes. It's a mouth ripped open, it's a tongue
                                                that
                                                    lolls.

The truth is in hiding, it's scared, it's weak.

You see, I've been waiting so long
                              for my chance to speak.

WAY BACK THEN – YEAR TEN

ONCE UPON A TIME

Imogen sat down next to me.

"Hey," she said,
"Joe, show me your notes?"
Tongue between her teeth,
she sat and copied every word –
my homework too –
then handed back my book with a smile.

"Thanks, babe," she said
and I caught the smell
of mint and roses
and something else.

Imogen was in my form.
The new girl,
who didn't mind the spotlight's shine
every time a teacher asked her for her name
her London voice
sounded posher than mine.
She laughed and didn't care
when someone took the piss and called her

snob —
she flicked her hair,
"Yeah?" she said.
        "Prove it."

She sat next to me again that day,
"Hey, Joe," she said and nicked a chip,
leaning across me to talk to Ryan Wall
who was on my team and played in goal.
I nearly gave her all my dinner,
nearly said, *here, go on, you finish it,*
instead the blush
that flushed my face
made me so hot
I couldn't even look up
and meet her eye.
I legged it outside —
trailing fire.

After that I tried
so hard to understand
everything
before the teacher even taught it —

I read books
actual books,

the librarian nodded when I snuck in before school
when no one was around to take the piss,
I sat in the corner
gulping down
thousands of words:
particles and plateaus
algebra and allegory
bloody poems
and
stories,
tragedies,
comedies.
I was going to get expert
just in case
she needed me to explain
something
inexplicable –

like why I couldn't tell her
how she made me feel.

There had to be a word for that –
some biological term
that explained
the way
my tongue tied itself up

in knots –
tight like the laces on my football boots –
my words
frayed and tattered
and got stuck
before I could
present them to her
in a perfect bow.

SO NOW

I'm outstanding at biology
and geography, maths and English too –
top of the class.

And all because
I have traced
the particularly perfect web of Imogen's veins
on the insides of her arms,
and on the soft skin of her neck,
and over her ribs,
and back, and body,
so many times

that I could
make a map of her from memory,
turn her into a sonnet,
calculate her heart rate down to its last beat.

POPULAR

I burned
and Imogen was the match
that set me alight –
I knew how close she was, how far away,
and wondered if she'd talk to me again –
I heard her voice echoing up and down the corridors
as she sang her way through school.

Small.
Fierce.
Head high,
dancer's stride.

Sheet of long hair,
hot in the sun.

Pure alchemy –
everything began to glow –
as Imogen wandered around our school
striking gold into its bones.

Imogen wore headphones everywhere
and didn't seem to care
that no one else was dancing.
I watched the other girls
watching her
and then
coming to school in
matching messy buns,
crowding round her table at lunch,
asking her what it was like down south
in London,
if she knew
the queen.

I thought that if I liked a girl,
maybe she'd be the one I'd choose.
But I'd been happy with my mates and the way my life
ticked over, like an engine, newly tuned.

If you're forcing me to describe myself, I'd say I was
an all right looking lad, fairly shy,

(my mum says she'd die
for my eyelashes, Bambi she called me
making me run upstairs, ears burning).

I wasn't sure what to do with girls
my football was all I needed,
I'd made the local under-sixteens.
And I had my mates, the lads,
Danny who played defence,
and Naz and Saif and Jack.

We had granddads who'd built up this town
years before we were born,
and our fathers worked together
outside in all weather.
We knew about tough,
about strong.
It was just a matter of living up
to what we were supposed to become.

I stared in the mirror without my shirt
and waited for a man to emerge.

FIT

"What are you gawping at?" said Annie,
neighbour, and friend from way back,
(our mums had been on the labour ward
together,
we'd been born
almost at the same second,
never mind the same minute
or month).
"You don't fancy her, do you?
God, you're predictable, Joe –
is that why you're going for the
boy band hair?"
She messed up my trim –
I'd got my mum to cut it nice –
I swore, tried to style it back right.
"Jesus, Joe."
Annie shook her head,
"You've got it bad."

ENGLISH

"So, who'll read Juliet?" Miss said.
And Imogen's hand shot up.

No one else volunteered.
I smirked at Dan.

"And now we need our Romeo,"
the teacher smiled
and all the lads squirmed.

I stared out of the window,
swung back on my chair,
that was my first mistake.

Because when the chair slipped
and I half tumbled to the floor,
the teacher decided

I was the perfect choice.

IT DOESN'T MAKE SENSE

I stumbled over oxymorons,
let brawling love's heavy lightness
make a fool out of me.

The other teachers knew not to ask me to read aloud,
that it wasn't fair
that I'd struggle and splutter,
drown on air.

Miss let me stutter on
and Imogen was patient,
waiting with a smile –

not laughing while I mangled
poor old Shakespeare's rhymes.

SHARED SONNET

Imogen put her palm to mine, and then Miss said,
"Come on then, Joe, this is the bit where you
get to fall in love. You're not dead yet,

you know? Make us believe your love is true."
The class roared. I said
my line, and Imogen stepped closer in,
whilst I lost the words and lost my head
somewhere in between the shrine bit and the sin.
Danny whooped, Imogen smiled, mouthed the phrase
I'd failed to say. And then it was time.
The room glittered, sunlight made us brave
as she put her mouth on mine.

"Ahem, if you don't mind," Miss said. We pulled apart.
That's when it happened; that was the start.

UPROAR

The classroom exploded in whistles, shouts
and my face exploded into heat –
lava flooding my cheeks.

I stepped back,
gave a bow,
trying to hide the

                                          where.
                                      every
                               and
                          there
                     rushing
                  blood
              had sent
           that kiss
        pants –
     in my
hardness

Shit, I hoped she hadn't seen.

Imogen smiled, shrugged and spun
back to her seat
like this was just any old Monday.

WHEN YOUR WORDS

are never good enough
you learn to accept defeat
and keep your mouth shut.

But when I'm on the pitch,
at a match
chasing goals,
the fastest there –
     lifted up
          onto the air
             like my feet are winged
and I'm flying through worlds
outwitting, tricking
         opposition
then I know
there's something
I can do.

Every week, I played
for the thrill of it, for the goal-scoring,
match-winning buzz.
I knew there'd be no better feeling –

until one day, not long after that kiss,
Imogen came along to watch.

"SHE FANCIES YOU,"

Dan said, and I kept my head down,
concentrated on the ball,
on my feet, on tackling,
dribbling, keeping my head in the game.

But my smile was in my belly,
in my throat, in my eyes.

Dan nudged me.
"Ask her out, go on."

Maybe he was right,
maybe she liked me
maybe it was time.

Year ten when Imogen joined our school
everything I thought I knew
split open, even the sky
had never been so blue,
grass licked my feet
its tongue hot and panting
as I ran on the pitch
chasing goals
that afternoon.

HOW?

That night
I wanted to ask my dad what to do,
but I knew he'd laugh, make a joke,
and Mum would purse her lips and say,
"No one's good enough for you, Joe."

People thought
I was the kind of lad
who knew how to talk to girls,
that I'd found my voice and that looking a fool
didn't worry me, at all.

Monday morning, just before the bell,
Dan gave me a shove.

I almost landed in Imogen's lap.

"W-   ill you go   out with me?" I said —
which were not the words
I wanted to use,
and were in fact the words
I'd planned to avoid,
because they made me sound like a kid
who'd never been on a date before,

which is what I was, of course.

But they were the words that came out first.

FIRST DATE

In the end I decided
that
ice-skating
would be good.
and when I asked,
she smiled and nodded,
said she liked it, was a pro.
(It was another thing I didn't know
how to do – but I gave it a go.)
And although she may have exaggerated, just a little,
sliding herself into the side of the rink when she went

too fast –

she held me up, when I wobbled.
It was a good excuse to grab her hand,
and she didn't mind when I didn't let go.

BLESS YOU

After our first date,
(which, as it happens, was pretty cool –
I could skate it turned out,
and spun her round and round,
until we were dizzy, and desperate
 clinging close, laughing like fools)
I thought I'd caught a cold.
Sneezing and coughing, a bit of a fever –
Mum even said I should stay off school.

(But actually, Imogen, I'd just caught you.)

SECOND DATE

Was a party at Imogen's place –
her mum was away –
there'd be no one home,
no one for miles,
no one to hear us going wild.

I cut my face on Dad's razor –

that aftershave sting.
I'd saved up my birthday money
and bought new jeans.

"Be careful, son," Dad said,
as we pulled up outside
the big smart house,
and stared up the drive –
thick gravel, tall trees either side.

FUN

Someone had beer,
someone else had weed –
I didn't like the way that made me feel –

my lungs on fire,
              and the room
                            a centrifuge of faces.

Imogen had moves,
she shimmered,
the music pounding in her.

But I could only shuffle,
embarrassed,
arms swinging like heavy branches.

I stood outside with Dan
in a garden winking with blue lights,
and we watched kids stumble,
drunk,

laughed at
someone throwing up.

Later we all jumped into her pool,
my clothes floated around me, heavy balloons.

And then I found her, under water, holding her breath
hair fanning out around her, a mermaid in a sequined
                                                    dress.

MOVING ON

"So am I your girlfriend then, or what?"
Imogen said it with a smile,

                    bumped her shoulder to mine
                    as we stood on the corner after school.

I scuffed the kerb with my shoe,
and pushed out a *yes*,
imagined my cheeks colouring red,
and invited her home for tea with my folks.

Mum banned us from going up to my room,
and it was awkward, sitting there,
Dad in his chair, grinning,
while we pretended to watch TV,
plates balanced on our knees.

"Let's go," I said, shovelling down my beans,
and we legged it, ran laughing down the street,

ended up in the park, standing up on the swings,

the metal jolted and juddered, then lifted me,

I began to swoop,

could see the roofs of our town,

and almost tasted sky.

I didn't need a parachute, or a net,

when I jumped –

for a moment

I had wings.

FALLING

Birds circled,
clouds shifted
and the sky was clear.
Our town was the centre
of the world, the universe turned
on a pin, set here.

"What's your favourite colour?
Book? Film?
Capital city?"

I pulled answers out of
air
and grinned when she said –

> "Yes! Paris, of course!
> What? Blue? Me too!"

I wondered how
she already knew
me.

TIME

passed slowly when she wasn't around,
and I shook my watch
        wondering why the hours
had   stopped.

I paced my room
(which felt too small –
walls inching, creeping closer,
body twitching, growing, itching)
until Mum yelled at me to quit,
and sent me out
to burn off whatever it was that was eating me up.

No matter how fast I pedalled,
my blood still hurt

and all I could think of was

Imogen's voice,
her lips
her eyes.

But mostly   her skin
next to   mine.

NOW

I STILL FEEL LIKE A BOY

– a kid
too young for this.
I feel skinned
and stupid,
as the lawyers talk about me.

The prosecution step forward

                         and lead us along

            a twisting path

                                    that weaves
                    through

        the rights

                                        and wrongs.

(but I'm on my own, criminal now –
no girlfriend beside me,
no hand reaching out
to anchor me,
rescue me
hold me, tight.
I'm here on my own
and I know how this goes,
I'm the lad who's a killer.
I'm that stupid sod: Joe.)

IT BEGINS

Prosecutor
knows how to prosecute
for sure.

He   rolls   out   his   words   like   rocks,
building   a   wall   impenetrably   high,
and on each stone is written a crime   of   mine.

I hadn't thought it would hurt
to be summed up like *that*,
for him to say how clear it is to see
that I must not be allowed to walk free.

Maybe he's right —
what you might call a perspicacious chap —
a man who can see right through
my new suit, shiny shoes, and all that crap.

Perhaps he's seen
right into my mind
and knows I dream blood
and death every night.

I guess he's used to the criminal type.

To him I'm a face,
I'm a body — six foot —
I'm a lad who can't smile,
a thug who's broken the rules.

If he knows anything,
then he knows that it's time
to see justice done
and face the truth of my crime.

"Mr Goodenough caused a death –
driving recklessly fast –
and his victim's family deserve
to see him punished at last.

We need to send out a message
to the world outside
that dangerous young men
will pay for their crimes.

It's time for the evidence."
Now he gestures wide,
a theatrical flourish
gets the jury on side.

He has witnesses plenty
so much to reveal.
He will tear this case open,
nothing will be concealed.

"You, the jury, must wait,

listen carefully, be sure
that your verdict is the right one:
a woman is dead, after all."

He'll tell them all about,
my damning failure to deny;
he has evidence galore
that I've told many lies.

We'll hear statements, and proof
to make the truth shine,
voices will speak up

like the one in my mind:

"It's your fault, Joe,"
it says,
it knows.

"NO,"

my dad calls, from far away.
"Just hang on, you'll prove it, you'll have your say.

Don't give up now, Joe, come on, be a man,
Your mum needs you at home; do what you can.

Just be patient.
Wait.
Your time will come.

You can't give up, Joe –
We believe in you, son."

HERE WE GO

The first witness for the prosecution
takes the stand. He's in his uniform,
but he's not that much older than me –

I've seen him before, at the match,
in the stands, cheering for our team.
I bought him a pint one night,
down the pub – when I'd just turned eighteen.

And he was all right,
the night of the crash,
almost kind to me –

the copper
who arrested me,
didn't cuff me,
didn't touch me,

just read me my rights.

HE SAYS

that yes, I confessed.

(my thoughts in a mess)

he's sure I said it,
that I nodded my head.

"Officer Blythe,
can you be absolutely sure
that this man here,
Joseph Goodenough,
is the one you saw
that terrible night,
that he stood there in the rain

41

beside Mrs Stephanie White
and confessed that he was to blame?"

(I have no memory of this.
Just that body in the car,
broken
      and bleeding
and somewhere

in the distance,

Imogen   screaming.)

                "That's right, as I said
                it was Joseph
                right there.
                He knew what he'd done,
                he was gutted, to be fair.
                I took him back to his vehicle
                and I read him his rights
                and he nodded,
                he was calm,
                the lad didn't fight."

BODYCAM

We watch the footage
from my arrest –
I don't want to see it,
but there isn't any choice.

"You do not have to say anything."
(I have nothing to say,
anyway,
nothing, at least that will make this go away.)
"But, it may harm your defence,"
(the officer's lips move –
the officer
who's leaning over me
in the back of a police car
that I don't remember getting into,
who is under the impression
that I need to make
a confession)
"if you do not mention when questioned,"
(please don't ask me to lie)
"something which you later rely on in court."
(or to tell the truth –
either way I'm screwed)
"Anything you do say,"

(just sorry, sorry, sorry)
"may be given in evidence."

I DON'T KNOW WHO THAT IS

That Joe, in the film,
Joe, months ago –

he was a different lad.

I look smaller then,
and frightened.

Bullied by the wind,
the rain, the cold –
I did what I was told.

In that police car
I hunch and tremble,
weep and shake.

And the officer doesn't cuff me
as I admit that I'm to blame.

Our voices crackle, but it's clear it's me.
I stare at the screen and don't like what I see.

"Do you understand the caution, sir?"
I nod and shake and cower
and say,

                                        "Y   eah."

"And you realize what you've done,
that you've killed a woman,
right? The driver of the other car,

                        she's gone."

I nod my head again
and then
the court is ripped open
by the size of my howl.

I cover my ears, close my eyes at the sound.

HOME

We should have stayed at home last New Year's –

Never should have roared through unfamiliar streets

weaved down roads, and lanes, through places I'd
   never been,
should have stayed home, close to all I know.

Home is in heart beats,
I feel it here
the needle of the compass
marking me
inside my skin.
And my pulse pulls me back
to my mum and my dad –
to where there's gold in the bricks –
in the foundations, the plans,
where there's love in the tread, in the palms
of their hands.

MY MUM

sits somewhere close,
and I pull myself straight with the knowledge of that.

She is roots and blossom,
she is graft and strength.

Sad pillar who holds me high,
even though I've grown

too tall for her arms.

CROSS-EXAMINATION

My defence has a go
at making it shift,
but the copper likes his story –
this shit will stick.

"Officer Blythe,
are you completely sure
that when Joseph was arrested
he knew exactly why, and what for?"

> "Yes, he admitted it,
> Yes, he said.
> Yes, *I was the driver,*
> Yes, *I confess.*
> You saw it on the body cam,
> It's not hard to hear.

> And no, he wasn't bullied,
> No, he wasn't under duress.
> It was all above board
> *I'm guilty*, he said."

"And the girl he was with,
Imogen Harris,
Who was there when Joe confessed.
Was she also under arrest?

> "No, but she was breathalysed,
> and we had Joe's admission.
> Imogen was with the medics,
> she was in a bad condition."

JURY

Silent, of course,
they lean forward to get a good look –
hanging off the copper's words
they want a glimpse of the beast
who could drive like a maniac
through a dark night,

48

who could kill another person,
risk so many lives,
who could admit that he did it,
and then change his mind,
who'd start to wriggle and squirm
at the thought of his crime,
when he thought about prison
and didn't want to do the time.

LOCKDOWN

I can hear doors closing already,
clanging shut behind me,
iron heavy.

I can hear the chains, the rattle of keys,
the biting song of
those metal teeth.

Locks grind into place,
turning, sliding,
groaning – that's it:

there's no way out

> not now you're within –

the game's up, Joe,

> it's time to pay for your sin.

ROUND OUR WAY

it's not hard to find someone
who's been inside.
Could be drugs, GBH,
robbery,
knives,

could be just a stupid mistake.

"Whatever you do,
don't get banged up,"
said the ex-con who came to school in year ten.
His words stayed with me,
a burrowing worm,
followed me, stuck
in the maze of my brain.

It was an echo of my father
with steel in his eye

telling me to always do what was right.

FINGERPRINTS

My fingerprints are everywhere –
of course they are.
Why did I ever take that car?

The barrister tries to get the forensic guy
to say that the facts are
incontrovertible.

Traces of tyres
on frosty roads have been
measured.

Calculations have been done –
they read:
too many miles per hour.

At that speed we should have been flying.

We should have taken off,
soared up and away,
leaving the world behind us safe.

Where would we have landed?
How close to the sun?
Would the stars have consumed us?
Could this have been undone?

He reads out crash data:

"Vehicle speed:
one hundred and ten miles per hour.

Engine RPM:
one hundred and ten thousand
revolutions per minute."

He boggles our minds
with figures
then slices through the numbers
with the facts:

"In those conditions

and on that road
a safe speed would have been
thirty miles per hour.

The data tells us that the
vehicle hit standing water
and the driver lost control
which isn't surprising
given the state of the road."

"In your expert opinion,
was the driver
Joseph Goodenough
driving with due care and attention?"

A simple answer comes back:

                                                  "No."

THINGS THAT HAVE BEEN BROKEN

Speed   limits,
He   arts,

Pro   mises
La   ws

t h e r e
        a r e
                p i e c e s
                        o f
                            u s
                                e v e r y
                                    w h e r e
scattered dust,
                shattered glass,
                                wasted lives.

ARE YOU SURE?

My barrister takes over, and asks
if any of the expert investigations show
that he can be one hundred per cent certain

54

I was driving that night.
"Are there photographs?
Is there footage?
Any DNA that specifically ties
Joe Goodenough to this crime
In that place, at that time?"

        "His fingerprints are on the steering
           wheel,
        the handle of the door,
        his DNA is in the fibres of the car.
        Blood analysis positions him
        in the vehicle, at the scene.
        The car was not fitted with a dash cam
        device, but the forensics almost
        certainly confirm
        that, yes, Joe Goodenough was driving."

It's difficult to argue with his
expert view.

If Imogen were here in court
I would ask her what she thought.

Because she knows how to
leave a mark, how to put a scar into a heart.

I'd ask this so-called expert
what he thinks of the evidence

Imogen's left everywhere
on me.

Because right now
she's in my head,
too close, her bones grafted onto my own
just as she was that night
and all those months ago.

WAY BACK THEN – YEAR TEN

CONGRATULATIONS

Coach made me captain of the team.

I ran to tell Imogen,
but she was quiet, grabbed her bag.

"What's up?"

"Nothing, it's just,
good for you, Joe, I guess."

I messaged her later,
because she hadn't called,
or waited for me after school.

"What did I do?"

                                    The sound of her shrug
was loud down the phone,
it made me feel like
I'd made a mistake
and that I'd better make it up.

HER BEST MATE

Kiran said,
"Look, Joe, Imogen just feels insecure,
she thinks you like other girls,
so you need to do more
to show her how you feel.
Why don't you put a bit of effort in?"

I didn't really understand
what I had to do to prove
what I thought she already knew.

VALENTINE

I got her a card and a teddy,
a plastic rose that played a tune:
it made me laugh.

She stuffed it in her bag, her mouth twitched –
I knew it wasn't the right sort of smile.
"What did you want?
Some soppy stuff?" I asked.
"Why the fuck would I want a poem?"
She sort of laughed.

She wanted a flash mob,
a wall of roses.
Real proof,
quantifiable in
likes on Insta,
or money spent
that I was for real; that what I said, I meant.

How was I supposed to know?

She'd bought me a chain,
heavy gold.
I weighed it in my palm.

She fastened it around my neck.

We didn't speak
all that week
and when Mum asked me why, I told her.

Maybe she'd help me understand.

Mum's lips became a line.

"She's just a spoilt little sod, Joe.
I wouldn't waste my time."

SORRY

Came quickly after and when Imogen took my hand,
sat on my lap,
one thigh each side of mine,
I couldn't help but kiss her back.

We spoke into the night,
and planned how far we would go –

I said,
"You're beautiful, Imogen."

                              "Shut up, don't take the piss,"

she said staring at the mirror –
picking at her face,
tearing at her hair so hard I winced.

I tried to give her more words,
but I don't think she heard
anything I said.

REVERBERATIONS

Imogen's parents rowed.
She didn't like the sound
of things smashing
the loud endings that dragged on into the night.

Even though they'd divorced
her dad would show up
and everything would blow up –
he liked to make a battleground of her home,

set up camp
in the living room
drinking red wine, turning up the volume
as he listened to the news.

"I pay the bills," he yelled,
"this is my house."
And her mum went to hide,
to fill up her own glass.

One night we sat holding hands
on Imogen's bed,
startled by the slam of doors below,
and the smack of his shoes on the polished floor.

We heard her mum squawk,
and their voices
speared through the ceiling, into her room.

At Imogen's place
we tiptoed, careful not to be caught
and spiked with their pain.

We made our way out
and ran to mine, through rain,
through a deluge like a sea, we swam home.

"Hey, Im," I said, "you okay?"
but she was floating far away.

SEX

"You know men think about it thirty-four times a day?"
Im said,
reading off her phone,
stretched out on my bed.

No it was way more –
triple that, I thought.

We messaged at night,
"So – when?" I asked.

                    "When what?" she replied –
                    with a laughing face.

Next day at break
I caught her hand,
pulled her into the rain.

Getting drenched,
I licked her face
her lips, her mouth.

We kissed
and then,

"Soon," she said.

OTHER GIRLS

"Who've you been out with before?"
Imogen wanted to know,
pushing me round and round
on the swing at the park
where we'd wandered after school,
tightening the twist of the chains
so I'd spin
when she let go.

My first crush was a girl
called Suzy,
but that was in year six.

I liked that she was smiley
that she always shared her crisps.

My second crush was Amy
– science partner in year eight
when she brushed my hand by accident
I was in a state,
when we nailed the experiment
I thought it might be fate.

When Imogen said,
"Are you a virgin, then?"
I nearly lied and told her *no*,
but then she let me go,
and whooped as
I whirled round and round,
spinning out of control.

DATE

so, how about saturday?
but don't forget the condoms, okay

Imogen messaged
with a row of exclamations
and dancing hearts
and a photo of her
wearing not much:
just her knickers,
and bra.

DARK DAYS

That week
Dad fell at work.
At first I thought it was nothing much,
his balance off,
a simple matter of mistiming.

Turned out it was something worse.

Everything changed, like it can,
in a blink, a flash
of planets shifting,
the universe twitching, changing course,
a reminder from the gods that boys like me

find the sun, for all its smile, really does burn.

Bleak, dark March,
that Saturday,
sheet ice meaning no match.

My parents had been waiting to tell me
that he wasn't going to get better,
that Dad's body
had turned on him
when he was still young.

So I didn't want to see anyone.

"I'm gonna stay in,"
I said to Mum,
who shook her head
and told me, "No."

I dithered in the hallway
tears caught in the back of my throat.

"We have to carry on as normal, Joe.
Go out, have a good time,
go on, it'll be all right."

Maybe Mum just wanted me out of the way,
so she could talk to Dad
on her own,
without me there,
listening in.
It gets exhausting,

                                        whispering,

and trying to smile
when you just want to cry.

I wanted to ask
How long has he got then?
but didn't dare –
those sort of words weren't fair,
they're the kind of words
that cut out the crap
and my dad didn't need that.

So I got my stuff
and she dropped me off,
and I sat in Imogen's living room
saying nothing
really.

AWKWARD

Immie's mum liked my smile, my height, my hair,
she thought I was cute.
"You've got a right one there,"
she said to Im,
making me blush.
"He's a looker – a bit of a catch,
 aren't you, Joe?"
I shrugged:
"D-dunno."

That night she left us with money
for pizza, whatever,
and a flash of a smile, a cloud of sweet scent,
then disappeared off out with her bloke.

                    "What's up?
                    Are you okay, Joe?
                    Are you nervous, then?"

Imogen smiled, and took my hand,
hers was smaller than mine,
nails painted pearly pink,
a chorus of bangles jangling at her wrist.

I pulled away.

I felt huge next to her,
Mum said I'd grown,
measured me against the door
– I'd hit six foot before I was sixteen, she said,
me with my giant arms and legs.
"Gangly lad," Dad laughed,
shouting from his chair.

"Is your mum out all night,
did you say?"
Imogen nodded.

           "Yeah, but Stefan's in,
           Mum thinks he'll keep an eye on us,
           but he's not arsed.
           It's fine, be chill."

Imogen smiled,
I pulled in a breath.
I felt like punching something,
the air tight and tense.
I shouldn't have been
sitting there,
talking shit with Immie,
waiting for a snog.

           "Come on, Joe,
           I'm sick of this,
           the suspense is killing me,"

                              she nudged me,
                              "let's go upstairs."

I followed her,
we collapsed on her bed,
but I didn't really want to kiss her, I wanted to cry –
I put my arm across my eyes
and trapped my tears.

"I got bad news," I began,
she shrugged, rolled away to put some music on,
mess with her phone –
she laughed at something, thumbs moving
fast to answer a message,
then
pulled off her top, climbed above me,
bent to kiss me,
I pulled back.

I wasn't sure she'd heard.

We stared at the ceiling,   lay there side by side
                    getting cold
and the silence swelled   and my heart slowed.

I got up, pulled on my coat,

ignored her shout,
"Hey, wait, come back, hang on, please, Joe."
I charged down the stairs,
jumped the last five
pulled up my hood, walked home.

FRIENDS

We used to have a lot of fun,
we could make rainbows out of rubble.

Next day when Dan messaged to say,
Come over, Joe.
I got my bike
and cycled off to see him,
pulling wheelies on the icy road.

Annie showed up too, and the three of us
made popcorn, watched movies,
mucked around.
Better, now,
I turned off my phone.

ANNIE

"What's happening then,"
she said,
when Dan went to the loo,
"with your dad?
My mum said he was bad."

"Yeah Dad's sick –
they said he won't get well."
I kept my eyes down,
shoulders tight,
controlling myself.

"Oh Joe,
oh, no,
I'm sorry," she said.

And then she hugged me –
Hard.

I started to cry –
hadn't been planning on it
but she was being too nice.

"Sorry," I said.

"Mate, it's okay."

Then Dan was back

and I pulled away.

"Woah, you two –
Mate, what did I miss?
I thought you were shagging Imogen
What's this?"

"What's it to you?"
I moved away,
wiped my face.
Tipped the dregs of my drink
into my mouth,
shook my head.

        "Oh. I get it.
        Well, better luck with Annie,
        then, I guess…"

She threw a cushion in his face.
"Danny, you prick.
Imogen and Joe are all right.
It's his dad, yeah?
Don't be a dick."

        "Oh right,"
        Dan said.
        "Shit, sorry, mate."

I shrugged.
"Whatever."
What else could I say?

TEARS

Imogen was waiting for me
when I got home,
eyes red, blotchy cheeks,
sitting there on the sofa –
make-up in streaks.

Mum handed her tissues, and Dad frowned
as she hiccupped and stuttered
that she'd only come round
because I wouldn't answer her calls
and she thought she'd upset me,
but she didn't mean it, at all.

"Please don't hate me,"
she flung her arms round my neck.
Mum raised an eyebrow
while I patted her back.

IMOGEN SAID

"Sorry I upset you,
It's just I like you so much.

I'm sorry about your dad,
Please, let's make up.

I'm sorry for crying,
Sorry for being a mess,

I just really liked you,
You've got into my head."

And we spent hours together,
joined at the hip,
        the hand, the waist,
                the leg, the lip.

She said she liked being close,
that we didn't need to rush
into anything else,
it was cool – just us.

KISS

"My face is sore," Immie said,
"You scratched it all,
With your stubbly chin –
And look at my mouth –
I look like a fish."
We kissed, and laughed and
I pulled her onto my knee,
we squeezed into one seat
in the canteen.
Annie and Dan pretended to be sick.
Kiran held Dan's hand,
"Why aren't you like that with me?"
she said, slurping her drink.

Mr Burns wandered over and told us to
"Break it up."
Imogen rolled her eyes
gave the finger to his back.

Dan stood, burped,
"Mate, let's go,
practice, okay?
Coach'll go mental
if you're not there again."

I unstuck myself slowly,
and stretched, looked at her and
touched my fist to my chest,
to my lips –
and kissed
a promise   into the space between us.

HOLD ME

Dad got worse.
                "What do you mean?" Im said,
I shook my head as she babbled on –
                "You know what,
                I wouldn't even care if my dad was
                    dead."

I didn't know what to say to that.
                "It'll be okay, though, Joe," she said.
                "You've got me, I'll make you smile,"
she pulled my face out of its frown.
                "Hold me tight, Joe,
                it'll be all right, Joe,
                I swear,
                there's no need to be frightened."

I shivered against her,
breathing in,
knotting myself into her skin.

SICKNESS

My house smelled
of medicine, and sadness.

I didn't like the struggle
I saw standing behind every door,
reflected in every pane of glass.

Mum drew the curtains tight to lock away
a daylight that hurt Dad's eyes –
he slept too much

and I was scared he would die.

REVELATIONS

Imogen told me things about myself I didn't know,
                    "You're fit, Joe,
                    everybody says so."
I shrugged and blushed and then –
                    "And you're dead smart,
                    you and Annie, you're the cleverest
                    in our class."
That wasn't true,
I just tried, really, really hard.

I sat beside her in maths
And Imogen sighed.
                    "I don't get it," she said,
and I tried to explain.
She shook her head.
                    "Nope. Still not making sense.
                    I hate school, Joe,
                    it's a waste of time.
                    Let's get out of here,
                    go back to mine."

Imogen held on to me,
she grabbed my hand,
jumped limpet-like onto my back, my lap

I carried her, or caught her.

She kissed me
when other girls were near,
the press of her face on mine
was painful –
I didn't mind, in fact
I liked the crush of bone on bone,
the distraction of Imogen's hands.

She told me I looked good in blue
and we sorted through my stuff,
she made a pile of things for me to chuck.

PLEASURE BEACH

The world spun
one sunny Saturday
it picked up speed
and we screamed – tipped upside down
we glimpsed Australia, Asia
Antarctica, America –
a tumble of worlds at our feet –

that's how it felt as we flew, fast, strapped tight
on a rollercoaster
wild as the sea.

Later, swaying, soldered close
we lay on the beach,
baked like beached fish,
I licked the ice cream from her lips
blinded by the water in a still pool of sun.

Slow train home,
stopping – starting – stopping again
the tracks were hot.
"That was all right," I said.
"Yeah," she smiled,
"it was okay, I suppose."

NAN

Nan nudged me and asked,
"So, I hear there's a girl on the scene.
What's she like then, your 'Imogen'?
Posh, is she?"

I got hot,
cracked my knuckles,
gulped my tea.
Mum was doing dinner,
Dad was asleep,
me and Nan were watching TV.

"Er ... yeah, she's all right.
Like, nice, I guess –"

Nan laughed,
"I should think so.
Pretty, then?"

Words piled up behind my lips,
"Yeah, I mean, yes."

I LOVE YOU

I wanted to be the first to swear on it
to make the vow –
three words that had been stuck in my throat
for a while.

Mum was with Dad at the hospital
and I grabbed my bike,
cycled to Imogen's in the dusk
and waited on the step, out of breath.

She was home alone too.
"Mum's out somewhere, on a date,
Stef's at a gig,
so – don't just stand there, babe – come in."

We stood in the emptiness of her hall,
the house an echoing void.
My words thickened darkly in the silence.
I couldn't say it.

But she was waiting for me to speak.
I cleared my throat and
we kissed.
Long kisses
hot and soft and hard.
I buried my face into her neck
And muttered.

                    "What?"
                    she whispered, giggled,
                    squirmed,
                    "What, Joe? I can't hear."

Louder this time,
I told her straight,
"Um, yeah, so, I love you, Im."

Her face changed and she
looked away,
then looked back into my eyes and said,

                    "Damn. You stole what I wanted
                                        to say."

NOW

999

The prosecution play the call.

"Which service do you want?"
a voice calm, and cool.

"A-a-ambulance, shit, or police,
you've got to help –
help me,   please."

"What's the address?"

The court listens to my voice
disembodied, breathing fast –

Amplified it is broken,
chipped china, a smashed mosaic of sounds.

The snap as I stammer out my
"S-s-s sorry,"
and confess,
"I don't know,
someone's hurt,
we've crashed –
please,   just hurry,
we   need   help   fast."

Painful to hear the words
coming out so slowly
all the confusion,
all the mess
and I want to tear out my own throat –
wonder if those seconds wasted might have
given that dead woman hope.

"I don't know where we are,

out in the countryside
but somewhere near
the motorway, not far,
I can hear it, the traffic,
the M6, I think."

"Can you look at your phone, at Maps?"

I scrabbled in the dark,
fumbling thumbs, a frantic search,
rain in my face, in my eyes,
then finally finding where we were.

"Is she breathing? The casualty?
Can you please take a look."

But I couldn't.

I doubled over.
Shaking, sick.

MY BOSS

Stu's up there, I've not seen him in months,
not since he sacked me after I fucked up.

"Ah, Mr Stuart. Joseph Goodenough
was your employee.
Can you confirm the car he was driving
was one he worked on for you?"

I worked to help make ends meet.
And Stu was decent, he taught me a lot.

"I'm sorry," Stu said, calling me up,
"I have to give evidence. I'll do my best
not to make things any worse,
but I can't lie for you, mate."

        "Yes, I employed him, just part-time
        I know the family –
        Joe's dad's an old friend of mine."

"That aside, what this court needs to know now
is if this car in the photograph is one you owned?"

They show a picture of that

old Audi, gun-metal grey.

                    "Yes, we were working on it,
                    it was one from the shop."

"Did you give Joseph permission
to drive the car that night?"

                    "No, I didn't. I can't lie."

"And was the car roadworthy,
this car that he drove?"

                    "Not one hundred per cent,
                    not exactly, no."

"And would Joseph have known this?"

                    "I would have thought so."

"But he took it,
and drove it –
how can that make sense?"

Stu doesn't answer.
I lower my head.

"FOCUS,"

Dad said this morning, before I left –
"just focus

on coming home,"
he said, catching his breath.

I wish he were here.
And I grit my teeth against the sway of pain
that threatens to floor me.

But there's a sick roll in my belly
and acid in my gut
– it's been there for ever,
burning my throat –
I am covered in holes,
a leper, missing parts
and I'll never be whole –

not now I've been halved.

FIGHT BACK

Stu tells them I'm reliable,
when my barrister asks,
decent, good family – the lot.
But it looks like the jury have had it –
they've switched off.

The old guy's asleep –
well his eyes are shut –
and the woman who's pregnant
shifts around in her seat.
It was pretty conclusive,
even to me –
on top of everything else,
there it is: I'm a thief.

RECESS

I need to pee,
lock myself in a cubicle, sit down
and stare at the wall.

I want this done.
No more digging,
gouging out the past

like pulling rotten teeth from
a bleeding jaw.

Why doesn't anyone see the gaps, the holes,
the blood and the guts and the aching bones?

I can't stand the wait, can't take the test.

If I held up my hands,
said *I'm guilty* –
what then?

DEFILED

It's true what Miss said at school
when we did Macbeth –
about the guilt,
it stains.

I stand at the sink
rinsing my hands,
scrubbing the skin, rubbing it raw
like I want to see blood.
I glance at the door
and back into the glass.

Imogen's wavering there.
She smiles that old smile –
and holds out her arms

like I'll fall right back,
into her heart.

ESSENTIAL

Once she looked at me
and I wanted her to look again,
to flower for an instant in
the sun of her gaze
before I faded back into the grey,
curled up
tight and dark
when she pushed me away.

I needed her words to
tell me my worth,
needed her eyes to tell me
I was hers –
needed her hands to
touch me into
shape,
needed her heart
to beat me into
life.

"Joe, can I talk to you?"
she said, when she called last night.
I knew what she wanted –

her voice is an echo I can't leave behind.

MAN UP

"Everything okay?"
my solicitor says

and I nod
and go to sit back down
in my glass box,
where I'll pretend
not to shake
so the official beside me
won't notice I'm weak.

But now I'm wondering
what I should say
if it would make a difference
if I said I'm in pain.

But I have no blood, no proof –
at least I'm alive
my heart is still beating –

compared to my victim, I'm fine.

And the law doesn't wait
it's not bothered about tears,
so I swallow back my scream,
stare ahead, face my fears.

STRONG

When I dragged Imogen's body out of the car
and carried her clear of the wreck,
held her hair as she retched.

When I held my mum's hand when the officer read
    out
the charge sheet, that detailed my crimes.

When I helped my dad
when he fell, let him lean his shoulder to mine.

When I changed my mind and said
Not Guilty.

Was I strong enough then?

LAWYERS

They like to argue,
bandy,   play with words.

Quibbling,   quarrelling,
                            querying,   questioning.

They bat back and   forth with the judge
and I stare   at the match
as they argue

                                            evidence,
admissible or not –

                        their sentences are long
and twist around the point,
                        and my story can't get out

                of   this
                    snaking

                     pit
                          of
                               words.

NEXT WITNESS

It's a low blow
to bring out friends
of mine.
I have to say though,
I'm not surprised.

Although Kiran's not the type
to tell lies,
or at least
she wasn't.
She used to be all right.

Imogen's best mate
and one of mine
back in the day
when we were buddies, a gang.

Her big brown eyes
freewheel
around the court.

I try to catch her glance –
(But why? What for?
To smile and say, *please
don't do this to me*?)
but she's blinking too fast,
her mouth opens and shuts,
she gulps and
then,   nothing comes out.

Until,
eventually
she manages to say:

"Joe and Im,
they were like
the couple everyone wanted to be,
we shipped them so hard,

and all this
it's just
so awful, I mean –

Yeah, I was there at the party
when they had that row,
and I saw Joe drive off –
it sucks, okay,

Because I know she loves him,
I swear,
she really does

And no one wants to see Joe
go to prison
none of us

want
that."

THE BARRISTER SAYS

"Let's try to be a little clearer shall we,
Miss Sawar?

You saw Mr Goodenough
drive away from the party?"

She looks down, examines her hands,
then back up, straight at me, at last.

                    "Er, yeah,
                    yeah, Joe, I'm sorry, I did."
"So Mr Goodenough was
driving, you're certain of that?"

Her eyes get bigger, she blinks again,
maybe she's going to cry,
but I know what she plans to say.

                    "Yeah, I definitely saw him
                    driving, I swear –
                    Joe drove Imogen everywhere."

"And could you describe
the events of that night,
before the terrible crash?
What happened at the party
between this pair?"

                    "Um, sure, so,
                    we were having a good time,
                    but Imogen was upset
                    and they were falling out –
                    Immie had told me he kept on

99

being horrible like that,
you know, not calling her
or making her think
he liked Annie,
he said he was busy –
that sort of thing.

But she really loves him
and he gave her a ring
so we thought it was fine –
I know Joe didn't mean
to do anything bad.
Please, that's all, that's it."

"I see.
Now, would you agree
That Joseph Goodenough,
Your friend,
Had a habit of being reckless?
That he lost his way?
That he's the sort of young man
Who would risk
Someone's life?
That he had a thing for danger.
Tell us, what do you think?"

RISKS

We've all been stupid
some time,
haven't we?

All done things we've regretted?

I don't think this is fair,
I think it's supposition,
and whatever Kiran says
I wish they wouldn't listen.

KIRAN

What does she see
when she looks at me?
Someone finished, screwed up,
diminished, done?

And yes, she says it aloud,
how I'm not the person
I was once.

"Joe was the one who was supposed
to do well,
to fly, like the aeroplanes he made
and fired across classrooms."
She smiles
and for a moment
I think it's going to be okay.

"He was a bit of a clown,
when we were kids –
he liked messing around,
but he wasn't a mad lad,
not one of the bad lads.
He did well, he was clever,
and he was always just nice –
He smelled of fresh air
like he'd blown in on the breeze,
I liked that about him,
the rush of his run,
looping the loop
he'd zoom in
with this amazing grin—"

"Miss Sawar?
If you could answer
The question you were asked.

> Is Mr Goodenough the sort
> of man
> you can trust?"

"Yeah, like I said, Joe's not bad,
he's not daft, not all the time –
he'd never hurt someone
it's not his style."

> "But Miss Sawar, are you sure,
> That Joseph wouldn't
> Sometimes lose his grip,
> That at times he could
> Take unnecessary risks?"

"Well, yeah, I suppose,
but we were all the same –
I mean there's not that much to do
round our way."

WAY BACK THEN – YEARS TEN AND ELEVEN

FORGETTING

Reality got tough,
and parties got wilder –

it was good to go out, to shake off
the dust that clung to my clothes,
particles of worry, atoms of fear.

Sober or drunk,
we'd gasp and grasp lungfuls of each other,
fistfuls of skin,
flesh hot and sweet
panting in the street
drinking up her colours
evaporating into

                              s   t   e   a   m.

COUNTING DOWN

Time slowed –
at school minutes stuck

glued to the clock's face,
sticky and fat with exhaustion.

We urged them on,
willed seconds gone

while the rut of minutes,
that glut of hours, choked us quiet.

We sent messages that said:

you're fit
i want you
let's go back to mine   *you're hot*
                                          i love you
                                          what, right now?

and read them under the desks –
phones flashing fast
semaphores of desire.

I gave up
and smashed the clocks,
we got out – ran riot.

IT HAPPENED

We first slept together
under a carpet of coats.
I don't remember who made the first move.

I'd been lying there, quiet,
trying not to take up
Imogen's space
not to invade
too close,
just in case
she thought
I had ideas,
(of course I had ideas).

I reached out
into the heat between us,
pulled her beside me,
breathed in her air.

There were other bodies
lying in heaps

tangles of people
passed out, asleep.

We kissed
a lot,
then I got on top
unzipped my jeans.

We struggled,
and shifted, breathed

a cocktail of kisses into the dark –

Drunk – I didn't last long,
came hard and fast –
"Shit, sorry," I muttered,
she curled up close,
"It's fine, Joe."

When we awoke
I saw the sky in her eyes,
light beckoned
and we crept outside
picking our way
through
     the piles
          of sleeping bodies
               tiptoeing
                    into the dawn.

We gulped the light
and golden, shining, we ran home.

IMOGEN'S DAD

"He wants to meet you."
Imogen strode ahead,
"He'll take us out
tomorrow night
for a slap up meal, he said.
I don't want to go,
but we've got no choice,
God he's such an idiot, Joe.
He says he needs to know
what's going on."

"What?"

"Sorry. Yeah, I know.
So annoying, but
please, will you come?"

Imogen pretended to smile,
and I went home
and stared at my stuff –
my house, my dad –
and wondered how
I was supposed to act.

IMPRESSION

"Look at you,"
Imogen laughed at me.

"What?" I asked, pulling at my shirt,
smoothing my hair.

"Nice," she said.
She sniffed my neck –
"You've gone all out, Joe,
Who are you trying to impress?"

Mouth dry, I followed her,
licked my lips,
tried to cough up an answer
that didn't make me sound like a dick.

If I said:
Just you,
Would that be the truth?

MR HARRIS

sounded like London
and he smelled like leather
and crisp twenty pound notes
fresh from the cash machine.
I said, "All right," and stuck out my hand,
trying to act like a proper man.

Mr Harris thought he was funny when he said,
"What's this you've got here then, Im?"
Maybe it was the way I spoke,
or my clothes,
I didn't know what it was
that made him say that.
Mum had said,
"Just be polite, be yourself,"
but he was looking at me like I was

something else.

Mr Harris grabbed Imogen
and kissed her, said,
"How's your mum?
Still drinking too much?"
He looked at my trainers,
assessed the rest,

"What have you come as, mate?"
I pretended not to know what he meant.

He led us to his car.
Sporty, silver, sleek and fast.
I trailed my hand over the bonnet,
wanted to ask
how much it cost, what speeds he'd hit,
if he'd let me sit,
in the driver's seat for a bit.

We slid into the back
Imogen twisted her fingers into mine
as he revved the engine,
"Nice isn't it, eh?"

"Yeah, mint," I said,
"kind of car I'd like, Mr H."

The man grinned, nodded,
as if he knew exactly what I felt.

FANCY

He ordered wine, swilled it round his glass,
then slugged it back.
He chewed his food fast,
and words and opinions rolled at us
like cannonballs.
He stared at Im, took her, then me, in,
started firing questions, tests I wasn't sure I'd pass.

"What's your dad do then, Joe?
And your mum?
Where do you live?
Where are you from?"
Blood burst in my brain,
my belly was water.
Did he think I was no good, a loser
not right for his daughter?

He winced when I said that Dad was sick,
and Mum did hair,
as if that meant they were thick.
I hated myself for a moment when I said
I wanted more than that, to do something big –
maybe football, or sports science
at uni, or study English, or maths.

I wasn't surprised when he laughed.
  "Didn't we all?
Sounds like you've got your eye on the ball.

What about this one then?"
he pointed at Im with his fork –
"I don't know why she even bothers
going to school.
And as for this dancing and prancing around,
fat lot of good it does, Imogen,
you can have the salad,
and no dessert."
He winked at me, like I was in on the joke.

"She's really good, though," I said,
but nobody heard
Imogen's chair screamed across the floor
as she got up,
"You can talk. Fat twat,"
she said and stormed off,
but he didn't care, too busy telling me
about his business,
the deal that he'd come back
up north to seal and how ambition
was a man's best friend.

The waiter took our order,
I asked for steak,
but Imogen, slouching back into her chair,
said she didn't want a thing.

"Not hungry,"
she stared her father down,
"I already ate."
sat back, arms folded,
eyes elsewhere,
didn't speak.

"WELL DONE,"

Imogen said later on
standing on the road
watching him roar away
towards the motorway,
back the way he'd come.

> "Darling Daddy thinks you're
> great.

Whoop-de-doo,
lucky you.
Hope you're very
happy
together, Joe."

CAUGHT

Sometimes we skipped school –
Kiran and Dan following,
like boats bobbing in our wake.

We led, they followed.

That day we went down to the lake
we should have been in physics,
but no one felt like measuring anything

other than the speed
of the sound of our screams

as we leapt

off the rocks

ignoring signs that said
Beware. Deep water. Danger.

COMMON SENSE

Barbed wire and broken fences
should have been a clue,
but kids had been coming here for years
when it got hot,
too hot to think and sweat and swot.

Imogen dared Kiran to jump.

Who'd have thought the water
would have been so cold?

Kiran disappeared.
Seconds passed.
We waited for her body to break the surface,
to come   leaping back up.

I raced down there,
jumped in and

grabbed her
by the hair
and dragged her
free.

THAT SUMMER

Imogen was away for weeks and weeks –
a fancy holiday was the sort of treat
her dad gave her to make up for
other things.
I stared at the photos on her feed and felt
our worlds sliding apart –
didn't know if I could keep up,
or if I'd already been left behind.

I didn't know the other smiles laughing close to hers.
I didn't know the arms that trailed
around her waist,
I didn't know what to make of all
the hearts, the likes, the faces.

I spent the summer down the park with Annie, Kiran
    and Dan,

Jack and Naz,
and the rest of the lads,
we had a laugh,
messed about on the roundabout, the swings,
kicked a ball most days –
dreamed of the Etihad, and scoring big.

We had skies, at least,
and watched the night closing in.
Dan brought a speaker, and we fell into the noise
and it felt like something
somewhere, not so far away, could be ours.
I watched Kiran kiss Dan,
Annie took my hand, and the darkness spun.

Imogen came home golden brown
and smelling of the sea, the beach.
I thought I saw seaweed in her hair,
shipwrecks and starfish in her eyes
and the hot deep blue of Caribbean skies.

Imogen brought me home a bracelet made of shells,
and I wore it for a day –
then the thread snapped,
and though I collected the pieces
I couldn't set them right again.

SIXTEEN

My sixteenth birthday –
coat already on,
I blew out the candles on my cake,
kissed my mum, and turned to go.

Imogen had a bag
slung over her shoulder.
Mum didn't hear it clank
and clatter
as we walked out into the
golden September dusk
her voice followed us, fading,
"Have fun. Happy birthday, son."

It had become our thing –
to get a bottle,
two or three,
maybe, if Imogen could smuggle
them out without being seen.

We'd get pissed on a Friday night
or a Monday afternoon,
sit in the park, in the dark, in the light
and watch the stars, or the sun –

and drink until we felt wiped clean.

I was trying to stop the dreams
that made me wake, drenched in sweat.
Dreams of Dad
alone, weak, taking blows,
and me with my arms tied behind my back.

We had our stuff to forget,
and this made it easier
to begin.

"Happy birthday, Joe,"
Imogen said,
and she passed me the bottle,
then I lit her cigarette.

Kiran and Dan were there
when we got high,
when I rolled
the spliff for Im to smoke
when she took a drag,
and we laughed as she choked.

Kiran was there
when we set the night

alight,
with a stray spark.

I think Kiran's the one who dialled
for help,
no one ever found out
who started that mess,
the fire that burned up the grass,
set alight to the hedge.
No one knew all the things we did –

we never confessed.

STRIP POKER

Sitting in Imogen's den, in the dark
candle-lit,
dealing cards,
Imogen explained the rules
I shuffled a hand
she was talking so fast
I didn't understand.

For every royal flush,
I'd show her a pair.
For every full house,
I'd be stripped bare.

"What?" I said.
"What the hell's this?"

Losing shoes,
and socks,
my T-shirt,
jeans.

She sat there, fully clothed,
laughing at me.

"What's the point in playing
if you can't win?" she said,
kissing me,
then laughing again.

Kiran half naked,
Imogen laughing,
Dan putting on her bra
Imogen dancing –
snapshots, moments that blurred

and smudged
like oily fingers wiped over a lens.
We stayed up all night
crawled into the same bed
not sure who we were kissing
didn't care what we did.

CAUGHT

Dad caught on –
you can't get anything past
my dad.
He might have been sick
thinner,
looking older,
but he was still sharp,
and he could read me
even when I thought I was being smart.

"Where've you been, Joe?"

I came home the next afternoon,
eyes half open,

smelling appalling.
He got up,
slow – needing the stick
and I didn't dare leg it
away from him.
"Dan's."

"Don't tell me lies,
you've been drinking
I can see the signs.
Look at the state of you, lad.
Have you lost your mind?"

"I'm fine.
Don't worry
I can look out for
myself."

I edged up the stairs.

"You can't,
You're grounded
Until you can learn how to behave.
This isn't a joke, Joe –
You should be ashamed."

UNDER LOCK AND KEY

After that
they made me work:
school stuff,
reading,
and learning hundreds of facts,
solving equations,
masses of maths.
Phone confiscated,
Dad tested me
glasses perched
on the end of his nose
firing questions
and demanding answers.

"You could just leave,"
Immie nagged,
standing on the step.
"It's boring without you,
Joe, come on, come out.
Just walk out of there,
tell them to get stuffed,
come out with me.
I want to get drunk.
It's so boring round here,

I've got us some gear,
Joe, come on, then –
Joe, hurry up,
Joe – can't you hear?"

FUTURE

"What about the future, Joe?"
Mum said, forehead creased with deep lines.
"You could go to college,
if you give it a try.

We've got high hopes for you,
me and your dad.
You owe it to yourself
we won't let you go bad."

I got up early for my paper round –
swore I'd never drink again,
or smoke, or let my parents down.
Year eleven kicked in
with a punishment of tests.

After school there was the team, and training –
I started lifting weights,
doing extra work, revision stuff
the teachers said might help make up
for all the weeks I'd wasted.
My chores piled up,
into a stuttering tower –
I climbed and clambered up,
then slipped back down.

Imogen said something had to change –
she was wondering why I hadn't replied
to her ninety-ninth message that day.

Sorry, I'm knackered, I just need a kip.

Her silence lasted days,

                                   her turn to make me wait.

MOCKS

Imogen sat in the hall
her head on the desk.

I kicked the back of her chair
but she didn't sit up,
or even twitch.

I opened my own paper,
started to scribble answers,
pen moving fast,
then paused to rest
my aching arm.

When I looked back up
Imogen still hadn't moved.

I coughed,
shifted,
tapped my knuckles on the desk.
The invigilator frowned
and came to stand behind me,
waiting until I picked up my pen.

"WHY?"

"Why what?" Imogen said
as she strode ahead.

"Why didn't you even try?"

                "Maybe I'm sick of failing,"
                she said.
                "I guess that's not something
                you'd get."

DUMPED

Imogen piled the things she didn't need into bags –
tumbled clothes and make-up, unwanted tat.
I helped her to collect all her used-up things
and throw them away.

"It's called decluttering," she said,
looking at me.

She had stuff, so much that
sometimes we couldn't find the floor,
and she'd lose her notes, her pens, her thoughts –
confused about things she hadn't seen for months,
or something she said I'd said, but that she'd lost.

"Im," I said,
"this is a right mess,

I've got to go,
I've got a match."

"Typical," she muttered under her breath
and when I tried to kiss her
she turned her head.

WINNERS

The whistle blew
and I jogged off the pitch.
Dan bumped fists:
I'd scored the winning goal.

"Nice one," he said.

I showered, changed,
grabbed my phone and sent a message –
a picture of me and the lads
victory grins all over our faces.

A reply flashed back:

"Joe, we're done."

I stared, coughed,
shoved my phone back into my bag
and shouldered my way out of there.
"Joe, what's up?" Dan yelled,
I didn't stop.

PATHETIC

"Joe, love, what's wrong?"
Mum said, when I sat at the kitchen table and cried.

I showed her Imogen's text.

"But, I don't know what I did,"
Mum hugged me tight.
I was still a boy, though I looked all grown up,
Mum said, and I shouldn't let her hurt my heart.

"Oh, Joe, you're so soft,
I'd keep you like that if I could –
but you'll have to learn the hard way, love,
you'll have to toughen up."

"It doesn't matter," I pushed myself up
and shouldered away,
sat upstairs in my room lifting weights,
teeth gritted against pain, aching and
hating tears
I couldn't contain.

Trying to grow a pair
wasn't working.

ADVICE

"Move on," Mum said later,
"It'll be all right,
you're young
you're special,
you're kind and bright."

But I didn't hear her.

I got on my bike and pedalled fast,
so furiously my heart almost burst.
"Imogen, are you home?

Im, it's me, it's Joe."
I banged on Imogen's front door,
I shouted and yelled,
and I begged her, I stood there, pleading.

"Please, Im," I said,
"don't do this to me.
I love you, you know,
I'm sorry
for whatever I did."

PROVE IT

"Would you do anything for me?"
Imogen asked,
she'd let me inside
and I sat beside her,
smearing my tears all over my face
with the back of my sleeve.
and of course I said yes.

We sat in her bedroom,
I held my breath and Imogen nodded,

"Okay, then,
I think you should give me your
    password,
I'll let you have mine,
I'm going to check your phone
    each night."

"Why?"

"It's a trust thing, Joe,
no big deal, I mean,
unless,
you've got something to hide?"

NOW

COACH

He's someone else I let down
but I hadn't believed
he'd do this.
In fact, I'd thought he'd speak up
in my defence.

"Joe had potential," he says
all six foot three of him,
bulky in a suit
bulging muscles;
neck thick; tie loose.

"Who knows, maybe he could have been great.
But he threw it away,
didn't really have what it takes.
Couple of years back, he started to play up –
drinking, and smoking,
you know how these young lads get.
To be honest with you
he was a bit of a mess –
what I'd call a waster, a bit of a thug,
he'd turn up tired, hung over,
slow – I thought it was drugs.
It's sad, I know
that the lads round our way
don't know how to commit,
it's the youth of today."

I try not to listen, sink my head into my hands
although that's not a good look,
it's all that I have.

BOOKED

I've been booked before.
When you foul,
take someone down,
play dirty,
break rules and bones and noses,
then of course
there are consequences.

My barrister asks the coach if he ever reprimanded
    me.
If I was so bad, how come he made me captain of the
    team?

Coach answers with a shrug –
"That was before he threw it away,
made a mug out of me."

"Please, explain what you mean."

"Joe didn't show up,
he let down the team.
I'd made him captain, like you said – and it's an honour,
    you know.
And it was the final, our last game.

But Joe didn't show.
We lost the match,
The title,
The league.
I blame him for that.
It was the start, I believe."

BULLSHIT

He knows where I was that day –
I told him myself –
that Imogen needed me.

I'd taken her to the clinic because
we'd got in a mess,
her mum would go spare
and we couldn't confess
this stuff to her dad,
or my parents either.

Imagine Mum's face if
I told her what I'd done;
she'd want us to keep it,
she'd say it was a sin.

We waited hours to see someone –
I tried to make Im smile,
told her stupid jokes.
Her head on my knee,
she tried not to cry.

"I'm here," I said,
"I always will be."

She'd taken a test
in her bathroom that morning
hadn't waited for me
and I'd found her in tears –
a puddle of a girl
on the floor
and we'd stared at the lines
that meant positive.

Shit.
Neither of us could deal
with a baby.

We were still kids.

BABY

"I think it was a mistake," she said,
"Joe, we could have kept it, we could."

I couldn't lie and agree
but I tried to say I understood.

I reached for her, and touched her arm.
Small comfort, but I wasn't sure what else to do.

"There'll be another time,"
I said, "Oh, Im, it's okay, listen, I swear I love you."

She wept again, wouldn't stop
until she slept,
but in the middle of the night
I woke up
and found her in a heap
on her bedroom floor
crying for something
we'd broken
and couldn't repair.

Like an egg blown empty
A cord snapped in two

"It's gone," she said,
"forever."

And I told her she'd get over it,
It was the best I could do.

WORDS

They have words for boys like me:
Waster
Scum.

Imogen's mum,
after the crash,
spat in my face
told me that,
"You're not fit to lick
my Imogen's shoe.
She could have died in that accident
because of you."

When my teachers looked at me,
I knew what they wanted to say,
and even Stu, at the garage,

shook his head,
and said I'd let myself down,
and I'd better not come in to work again.

I said those words to myself
as I walked home from school,
back in January when Mum made me
start the new term
when all I wanted to do
was hide inside
under the covers,
crawl under my bed.
You're nothing,
worthless,
you'll never come good,
words gnawed at my head
and everything I read in the news
told me it was true.

Dangerous Yob Driver –
Dad on Disability –
Feral Teenage Thug
Pleads Not Guilty.

Pictures of me
hiding my face

when I first went to court
to hear the charges read.

Read all about it:
the papers know my name,
I'm fair game.
Joe Goodenough
aged eighteen,
who destroyed all those lives
for a night on the drink.
I made a good headline then,
and now, too, this past week,
they've even got my photo –
on my birthday, eight months since:
eighteen – drinking a pint,
stood outside the pub
face gurning with delight
having a cheeky smoke
white trainers, hood up,
I know what I looked like –
roadman,
scum.

I sort of hate that lad –
the one I used to be.
He knew sod all
about reality.

SPOT THE DIFFERENCE

The woman who died – look at her – see
She was twenty eight, ten years older than me.
They put a picture of her next to mine
holding her baby close, her toddler on her knee.

She was a very good person.

And I,

      it turns out,

            am not.

WAY BACK THEN – YEAR ELEVEN

LOSERS

Dan was raging
that I hadn't shown up,
the team blamed me for losing
that year's cup.

So I told him about it,

      what had happened to Imogen and me,

that she'd had an abortion
and that's where I'd been
when I should have been scoring big
for the team.

I thought he'd be sorry, or something,
a bit sad,
but he just kicked at the dust, spat,
shook his head.
And then he was like, "Joe, what the fuck?
How'd you know it was yours?
Joe, you're a mug."

The bang of blood in my ears
the burn of my rage
I shoved him.
Punched him.
Couldn't forgive what he'd said.

LIES

"Where's Imogen, Joe?"
"Oh, she had an appointment,"

I said to the teacher whose slow nod
told me he knew I was lying,
one raised eyebrow says a lot –
period four, maths – and this didn't add up.

I coughed, and tried harder
stutter slowing me down,
*"Think   she had an   emergency,
or something,   like that?"*

I took the notes she'd need –
photocopied my work
so she wouldn't fall behind,
I had her back
when she was too sick to show up,
or just fed up,
I didn't know what was wrong or
what I'd done.
I just knew she cried too much.
I called round after school,
her mum sent me up to her room.
"Im, hey, are you sure
you're okay?"
She didn't answer, shoved the work
onto the pile on her floor,
reached for my hand,

pulled me under the covers
into the dark.

"What is it? Come on, don't cry."
My words slid away from me,
lost amongst all the other mess.
I breathed in the smell of sleep,
and unwashed teeth, of her sweat
and wished I could lift her out of this –

I kept on talking, groped for things to say
to mend the break
patch up a wound I couldn't see.
"Im, we'll have another kid one day,
when we're married,
sorted,
it'll be good. Trust me."

"You promise, Joe?" she said
and I swore
on her life
that I would always make everything
always all right.

FULL ON

Dad gave me the talk
from his bed
one Sunday morning,
when he felt pretty good.

He sat up, the pillow bright white against his head,
and told me
that one day,
my love will be
the most important thing to me,
and that she'll be precious,
like that ring
he bought Mum for their anniversary.
Illness made him say
the kind of things
I thought I'd never hear
my dad admit.

"It sparkles, doesn't it, Joey," he said,
touching me on the cheek.
"Just like your mum,
and like you, lad."

"Right now though, Joe,

I'd say you're a bit young
for all of this.
Maybe cool things down –
take things slow –
you only get one heart,
son, best be careful, you know."

I shook my head,
He thought I was just a kid
He thought I was too young
To know what real love is.

TRIED AND FAILED

Imogen said she didn't care
about taking her exams.
"What's the point
if I'm going to fail?"

"Don't be daft," I said,
and packed a bag with my books –
I wanted to help.

But we ended up at the precinct,
wandering the shops.
Later she emptied her pockets
and shrugged.

"What d'you nick this for?" I asked
holding up a lipstick,
earrings,
a bag of sweets –

Imogen didn't answer,

she yawned in my face.

LEGACY

Imogen sat in class
notebook out,
it looked like she was actually making an effort
for the first time all year.
But Mr Jones
wasn't the sort of bloke
you could get one over on.

"What's this, then?" he said
whipping the journal out from under her nose.

"My last will and testament,"
she laughed up into his face,
"don't worry, sir,
I've not left you out."

She began to recite:
"To Mr John Jones,
my favourite teacher,
in honour of his personal hygiene
or lack thereof,
I leave
funds to provide
one can of Lynx;
a family-size bottle of
Head and Shoulders for his hair,
and one large spliff
so he can chill the fuck out."

Evidence confiscated,
Imogen isolated.
She didn't come in the next day
school could do one,
she said.

REPUTATION

When they called her name
and she wasn't there
the teachers rolled their eyes.

And if she did turn up
she wasn't quite so welcome any more.
These days most people
wanted to get on with the work.
Exams were looming
like icebergs
and we were on the *Titanic*.

She'd swallow an aspirin in class
and they'd say it was ket,
she'd take a sip of water —
"Miss, she's an alkie mess."

She'd trip over her bag,
        she was off her head,
she'd ask to go to the bathroom,
        she was on something else.

"Shut it," I said,
and jumped over the desk,

to face off with the fool
grin smeared like oil
and who was loudest of all –
Ryan Wall.

RYAN WALL

"So you're not bothered then?" he said,
laughing at my rage.

"What?" I answered,
heat rising up my neck and face.
"That I shagged her
the other night, dickhead."

Dan grabbed my arm
to stop my fist from swinging –
but I wanted to destroy him,
batter him into oblivion.

"She said you were done,
she laughed,
said you were shit.
I mean I wasn't that keen,

but she wanted it so,
yeah,
why not?"

REASSURANCE

"He's a liar, Joe,
he's taking the piss,
winding you up.
Just ignore him.

How can you think
I'd do something like that?

And even if I did –
how would that be my fault?
You've been ignoring me,
anyway,
and you're always revising.

I'm still waiting
for you to apologize
actually."

"What?"

But then came
tears running
shoulders shuddering,
mascara flooding her cheeks in filthy black streaks.

        "I'm so sorry," she said
        through the choking sobs.

A sixth former sauntered past, stared.
I put out my hand,
briefly touched Imogen's shoulder,
then she was leaning against me,
crying into my jumper,
her arms wrapped around me,
repeating it over and over –

        how sorry she was,
        how it wouldn't happen again,
        that she meant it this time, she
        promised on her life, and mine.

"Okay, all right, please,
don't cry any more."
She swiped at the tears, half laughed,
        "You forgive me?
        Say it, Joe."

     Her face serious now,
     eyes wide and intense
     she pinched my mouth in her
     fingers
and I agreed, "All right,"
because I needed her to stop.
I stepped back, she grabbed my hand.
     "So we're good?
     Everything's fine?
     Yeah?"

And I was about to say no,
no thank you, let's leave it, move on,
but I didn't.
I didn't.

And then the moment was gone.

SUPPORT

Because I bulged,
arms roped,
my abs six-packed

she liked me to lift her,
and loved the fact that I was so tall.

It was strange because
I usually felt

pretty small.

PROM

Tux on,
we were Hollywood fine –
Imogen gleamed.
I watched her shine
proud to have her by my side.
Mum took our pictures
waved me goodbye.
Then twenty minutes in,
Im grabbed me, said she was bored.

We left the party behind,
drifted away from my mates,
took the road out of town,
went our own way.

Imogen took off her heels
not stepping over the cracks,
she walked barefoot,
not avoiding the trash.

I said, "Im, jump up,"
and she hitched up her dress,
clambered onto my back
she didn't care where we went.

We ended up on the bridge,
that spanned the road out of town
that conduit to somewhere,
that linked north to south.

Imogen jumped down,
I rolled my shoulders, stretched,
but she was already leaning over the edge,
she yelled, threw her voice, then picked up a stray
   stone
and   careless

                         smiling

                                dropped it down

into the stream of cars.
"Stop it, Imogen, don't—"
I grabbed her arm,

"Let's go back, find the others."

But she said the party was done.

RESULTS

"It doesn't matter," I said,
"it's not a disaster,"
wanting to hide the news on my paper –
I'd done too well,
even better than I'd hoped.

> *"Easy for you to say,"*
> her face spelled danger.

She snatched my envelope
screwed it up,
threw it away.

> *"Did you do it deliberately*
> *just to make me look stupid?"*

I shook my head,
but she'd already gone –

I scrabbled to smooth the paper smart,
but the shine of all those numbers
couldn't last
and when Mum and Dad
asked what was wrong
I didn't know what to say.

NOT WAVING, BUT . . .

Another day, a week later, we went to the beach
and stood in the water –
the cold, grey Irish sea –
up to our knees
in escape.

I splashed her,
she squealed
and threw the water back into my face,
kept hurling handfuls
as clouds covered the sun
and I staggered in the waves.

I waded back to the shore

through soft sand and mud,
onto the pier –
watched the sky,
dried off on my hoodie,
waiting for a crack of light.

Like sentinels, statues of men
stared
blank-eyed and naked,
cast-iron hearts gazed
at the wide, wide sea
and through me.

I wished I felt their nothing.

We'd brought a picnic –
a bottle of fizzy wine.
I wanted us to have some fun,
remember how to have a   good time.

I watched Imogen
moving further and further
towards the horizon
towards the figures who were beyond our reach
and yelled,
"Im, Im, come back."

I guess –

she didn't hear me.

NOW

PROOF

I'm starting to believe
that everything I've ever done
is on someone's phone.

Maybe they've watched me eat
take a shower,
seen me sleep.

But this is a special edition,
more nightmares from the prosecution.

That party.
Happy New Year,
we'd screamed,
just minutes before.

I should have stayed at home,
watched telly with my folks,
raised a glass with Mum,
made wishes for the year to come.

But someone caught
it all
on camera,
Imogen and me,
like Marilyn and James Dean
starring in our own last scenes.

They press play.

Time to pray.

SCENE ONE

Imogen's blurred in the background,
and then there's me.

I squint to make it out,
look at my hands
around Annie's waist.

Cringe,
I'm dancing
like I'm wasted – no rhythm,
just a boy lurching out of time.

But it's true – I'm smiling
and I watch myself
lean in,

and see how Annie's eyes are on me
her face close, soft,

shit, it really does look
like something else.

WHAT WAS I THINKING?

That it was nice to be out,
to see my friends.
That maybe this year
something would change –
My dad would get better,
My exams would go well,

My mum would get a raise,
Imogen would chill.

I wasn't thinking
about breaking the law.
I wasn't thinking about
crashing the car.

I was just trying to have a good night.

SCENE TWO

Imogen comes over,
and Annie steps away,
I pass Imogen a bottle
and we dance,
as she drinks,
pulls me close,   *(whispering*
                                          something
                                                the jury
                              can't hear)

I struggle, pull back,
walk away, towards Dan,

who's beckoning me over,
from across the room.

Imogen follows,   (*they still*
grabs the back of my jeans   *can't hear*
to pull me up short,   *a thing*
she jumps on to my back,   *we say.*
arms round my neck.   *just see*

                                        me trying
                                to get
                                        away)

I pull her arms apart,   break free,   walk off.

I could have been kinder,
could have been patient,
listened, been careful,
should have been decent.

The court fills up with the truth of my shame.

The argument starts   see our twisted faces
Cacophonous mess   of music and voices

Imogen shoves me   I face her.
Imogen swipes   I grab her hands.
Imogen shouts   I step back

Imogen is small   I am tall

Imogen's upset   and I don't care.

SCENE THREE

It's all beats and bodies –
for a second the film blurs,
and we slip off the screen,
and I almost breathe,
want to believe
that's all they'll see.
But then I come into sharp focus again
with a yell,
as the music cuts out –
"What the fuck's wrong with you, Im?"

And she comes at me,
I catch her,
and she holds on
tight.
arms round my neck,
like we're saving each other,

then   (*then   she bites me –*

    I step back –   *do they·see that?*)

                    (*like always –*

                            defend

                            attack)

I put my hand to my cheek and try not to react
(*but even I'm frightened by the look on my face*
        I don't want to remember I felt that pain).

        "What's the matter, Joe?"

Imogen taunts,
and I try not to flinch,
wipe her spit from my cheek.

My fingers come back, covered in blood –
it's there, a dark stain, what's left of our love.

We've got a crowd,
it's my move –

so I shrug

                and try to act cool.

I swear and I spit,

I yell something nasty, act like a dick.

SCENE FOUR

Imogen crumples,
and I grab for her hand,   (*to try and explain*
                             that it didn't mean
                             what she thinks —

                             It's the middle of a party
                             she didn't want to come to,
                             "We should go home —
                             just be on our own."

                             but the lads had begged —
                             "Mate, we never get to see
                                you,
                             it's New Year's Eve,
                             don't bail again, Joe.")

"Hey, Immie,   please,
just listen   okay . . .
wait, ha   ng   on."

You can just make out
what I'm trying to say.

(I reach out – my words slow,

I can't bridge the gap,

can't grasp the space

as she steps back;

I'm poison, an infection

that she doesn't want to catch.)

SCENE FIVE

"*I'm done,*" she says.

(Then – shit –
that's it,
she's off, away.)

The jury see her run,
watch me follow –

(why won't she wait?)

I run
out of the party,

(away from my friends,
run through the shout of her voice
in my head,
towards her anger that waits:
sharp,

                    k
                      n
                        i
                          f
                            e -
                              e
                                d
                                  g
                                    e
                                      d)

"Imogen," I yell, into the dark,
until there she is, in the distance
and, I run towards her, and the car –

THE END

The film is done,
now there's muttering in court,

and shuffling, papers rustling.

                              The old lady
                              on the jury
                              with the beady bright eyes
                              is staring at me
                              as if she's seen
                              something vile.

And I want to stand up
and shout
that it's not how it looks –

                              but the guy with the beard
                              his hair in a bun
                              is shaking his head,
                              and folding his arms –

I swear I didn't mean to hurt her,
I never could.

Something has changed –
they think they know how it was.
They think they've seen
who I am –

and this proves I'm no good.

SLICED

The prosecutor's clinical, carving up
that night into portions of time

and they're eating it up, the jury,
though it really isn't right.

I watch my lawyer,
and wait for her to object
but she sits, arms folded,
doesn't see that I'm stressed.

I can't stand much more –
start shaking my head,
coughing, pulling my ear,
jiggling legs.

I want her to stand up,
to tell them "enough",
I'm being consumed
can feel those teeth in my flesh.

HORROR SHOW

The prosecution show pictures from the scene.

Feels like they should have said something,
like maybe seeing
images of
a woman **dying**
up there, on the screen,
in real life,
should have come with
a warning –

Her family are crying.
I can hear them
despite the glass around me,
despite the fact
that I won't look at their faces –

Their pain is loud.

I put my head in my hands,
can't bear to remember
the shatter
and shudder
the howling of metal,

that's been driving me mental.

It's in all my dreams.

Now I'll breathe to the sound of their screams.

MY DAD

can't be here
and I'm glad he's not watching this.

I'm glad he can't see his son
undone by the sight

of a judge in a wig,
of a jury who stare.

My dad's at home
waiting for me to be freed.

It's what he believes will happen today,
he thinks I'm brave.

Once he read to me –
no university degree needed

for the stories he told,
of boys who could fight monsters

and breathe fire of their own.
He's at home,

tied down by dying.
A machine does his breathing.

If I can be half the man he is

I'll still be more than most.

BREAKING

We stop for lunch,
and I sit opposite Mum
and try to cram
bread into my mouth,
chew

and think
and eventually spit
it out.

"I'm going to go down,
aren't I, Mum?"

She shakes her head
and we go outside
while she lights a cig.

Just for today, she's smoking again.

I want to be sick.

Her wrists are thin,
the bones in her ankles bird-beak sharp
and she's so breakable
it makes me want to   hurl

                   something

                         hard.

She doesn't deserve
any of this.

"Mum," I say into the smoke,

choking on my need to
hope.

"Mum, what do you think?"

"I think it's okay,
Joe.
Stay strong,
be brave, son."

She grinds out the stub,
and I put my arm around her,
while she lights another.

WHAT IF?

I give them what they want.
The jury.
The police.
Stephanie's folks?

What if
I do it.

End this now –
Change my plea, hold up my hands, admit it, say
I'm guilty?

What then?

I CAN'T TAKE IT

I ask for a break,
And tell my brief what I want.

"Are you insane?"
my solicitor says
when I tell her my plan.

"No.
No way.
We're doing well, Joe,
there's a long way still to go –
you can't give up,
you can't give in
you'll have to fight on
if you want to win."

But I know what's coming next:

Imogen.

PART TWO

BACK THEN – YEAR TWELVE

DRAMA

Imogen decided
that if the school wouldn't see her talent,
then she'd find someone who would.
I nodded, true, that was a good idea,
to branch out, blossom, and prove to the world
who she was.

She didn't come back to school,
into year twelve
when I signed up for A levels
she found a college somewhere else.

Imogen could dance and sing and act,
and I went to her first show,
no sign of her mum –
I sat in the front row,
on my own.

I knew her role back to front,
inside out, upside down –
You're amazing, I thought,
as I mouthed along.

We stood up to cheer
as they took their bows –
a standing ovation.
I was proud.

"This is Joe," Imogen said
afterwards, alive with the glow
of the spotlight,
the stardust –
all made up –
happiness made a difference,
I could almost taste it
and I smiled,
stood on the sidelines, with a drink
and watched her shine.

She introduced the leading men:
"This is Oliver, and Ben."
I shook hands,
and laughed at their jokes;
they looked surprised when it turned out I knew
what they meant
when they said
that Bertolt Brecht
had reinvented drama
back in the day.

I said, "Yeah,
Don't forget Stanislavski, though, mate."
That shut them up
and I raised my glass, toasting myself.

Later Imogen said I was paranoid –
that of course they liked me
and they were no threat –
                                    "Are you jealous, Joe?
                                    Ha – that makes a change."
I didn't get what she meant.

SOMETIMES STRONG

November.
Fireworks –
Imogen and I stumbled home,
a little bit merry,
not too much –
we'd been out on our own
to the big show in town –
and the world was all right
in that moment before

we turned the corner,
saw an ambulance at the door.

Panicked we rushed:
"Mum, Mum – oh,   shit, what happened? Please ..."
Men in green, at the doorway,
hushed tones, I stumbled near.

"Oh, Joe, it's okay,
Dad, he couldn't
catch his breath – chest rattling –
I was scared –
no hospital, I promise,
he's stable, for now.
You go on in, it's okay –
go up, leave him be."

I leaned against the wall
afraid of falling, sinking to the floor.
For a second I'd thought the worst.

Imogen held me,
"It'll be okay, Joey, it'll be all right –
it's nothing, don't worry – he'll be fine."
She wrapped me warm, in arms
thin, but tight

keeping my pieces together
that night.

MONEY

Sick pay doesn't last,
and paper rounds pay pennies.

I turned seventeen
and took a job pulling pumps,
polishing mirrors, cleaning screens,
the smell of petrol soaked into my jeans,
but Stu told me he'd teach me how to fix up a wreck,
and I wanted to know how to make broken things

work.

He said he'd teach me how to drive
and I raced his old bangers after hours
liking the speed, the roar of the engine,
the squeal of the tyres.

Imogen hung around the garage,
bored, she said,
she'd chew gum, or sing, paint her nails, run her lines,
and make me and Stu laugh

sitting at the desk, answering the phone,
pretending to do the accounts.

She asked me to go away with her
when the Christmas break came.

        "Joe, it's no fun,
        just me on my own
        Dad all over whichever woman
        he'll be dragging along."

"Stay here, then, don't go."

        "Come on, don't be a bore.
        Let's have fun for a change
        Or shall I ask someone else?"

I almost wished I could,
but I had to say no.

        "Don't be stupid," she said,
        "we'll pay, well,
        Dad will, if I say
        I want you to come."

"No, I can't," I said.
Not that year. Not then.

        She folded her arms.
        "Joe – give me a break."

I shook my head.
The look on Imogen's face told me
I'd made a mistake.

CHESS

I stayed at home
and set out the board, sat by Dad's side

Christmas songs on the radio,
Mum out at work.

We played long games
through wet December days.

Rain drumming on the roof,
living room air, thick and safe.

Dad took his time, and I watched
and learned through losing.

Sacrificing pawns, and rooks,
bishops and knights –

I couldn't see that
I couldn't always go backwards
to correct my mistakes,
couldn't see that sometimes there was a better way
to protect myself.
I'd be no good in battle, Dad said,
and I gave up and read to him,
instead, our favourite story from when I was a kid –
about a knight, and a monster,
on a mission
to save a princess. He smiled,
fell asleep just after he said –
"It's just a story, Joe,
remember that, mate."

I MISSED IMOGEN

I marked off the days she was away
and saved up enough
to take her out when she got home –
somewhere fancy, somewhere smart.

Last day of that year, Stu said he'd lock up,

and I ran round there

                                        late –

her plane had landed,
no time to wait.
Black under my fingernails,
rough hands,
and a head full of things I wanted to say.

She didn't like it when I touched her,
or the dirt on my face.
And I apologized for the fact
that I'd been working all day.

ROW

We didn't make it out
that night,
I stood on the doorstep
whilst she yelled.

            "It's not my fault," Imogen said,
            "that we don't see each other so
                much
            any more –

you and your football, A levels,
that stupid job –
God knows what else you've been
    up to
whilst I've been gone.
I mean, Joe, you've made it really
    clear,
what your priorities are."

I tried to think of ways she was wrong.
But it was true,
my hours were swelling up with other things
I had to do.
"I'm sorry –
can I at least come in?" I begged,

                         "No – I'm tired.
                         I'm going to bed."

OUT

Not long after that
my phone went –

Deep in sleep
exhausted after
studying late,

I almost didn't answer,
then I saw Immie's number.

Default setting disaster,
of course I thought the worst,

Grabbed the phone,
"Yeah, Im, what's up?"

"Joey, come get me,"
her voice was thick and hurt.

"Why, where are you?"

"Olly's place, at a party,
I don't feel too good.

Joey – I'm sorry,
it's the last time – I promise."

NEEDY

We went out with her new college mates
the next Friday night,
but that was the last time –
for a while –
and then I saw her, out,
in a club in town.

"Imogen," I yelled trying to make her hear
over the thump of the bass –
she was dancing, arms in the air,
eyes closed, in her own world.
I shouldered towards her,
and, leaning forward
my mouth brushing her skin,
said,

"Hey, Im, I didn't know you'd be here."

I had to shout to be heard
the darkness swallowed my words
and when she shimmered away from me,
I followed, held onto her hand.

We stood face to face,

I stroked her hot cheek
and said,
"I love you."

She answered,

                                          "Okay,"

like it wasn't,
like she wondered what I meant.

And I lifted my voice
yelled,
"So –
do you – you know –
still   love me?"

She shrugged, and closed her eyes,
and then smiled.

                        "Yeah, mostly, it's just
                            that sometimes you're so fucking
                                      boring, Joe."

"Clingy," she called it
when I complained
that she was dancing with the other guys,
again.

I tried so hard to be cool,
reasonable,
they were just friends –
and I left her to it,
walked away from the temptation
to say,
"Sod this, have it your own way."

I sat, on my phone,
by the bar,
and waited
until she'd had enough.

CHAUFFEUR

"You'll drop these guys too,
won't you, Joe?"
"Er, yeah, where d'you live?"
I didn't want to, though.
A thirty-mile round trip?
I put my foot down
and drove in silence
– this was taking the piss.

"All right, grumpy," Imogen said,
when they'd gone and we
   were on
our way home.
"Do you want money for
   petrol,
or come in – let's go to bed."

Her house was dark, and
she smelled of the club,
and I couldn't feel my fingers,
my skin,
I was numb.
My tongue
thick with questions –
Is this it, are we done?
I sat, elbows on my knees
listening to her singing and laughing at me.

Then she grabbed me,
pulled me up and off my seat,
jolted me,
shocked me, reminded me to breathe.

We kissed
and I held her face in my hands,

stared into her eyes
and said,

Nothing.

TRUCE

Face   to   face
I told Imogen

I couldn't take it.

She leaned forward, inched her
    hand across the space   towards mine
in the coffee shop heat
                        our fingers touched
        she held my hand,
and swore   on my life.

WHAT HAPPENED TO YOUR FRIENDS?

"Why doesn't Dan come over any more?"
Mum said,
"Or Annie, the old gang?
You barely mention them, Joe."

I shrugged, and told her I didn't know.

It was easier to stay in,
by myself,
just in case.

I told my mates it was because of Dad.
And when I saw Annie,
in her garden,
I nipped back inside.

I worked out in my room
lifting weights,

and waiting
for

something.

SUMMERTIME

We took a trip to London,
made our way the length of the country —
backpacks on,
the train spat us out into the heat of the day.

Imogen knew people who'd let us stay,
and the afternoon blurred
into evening,
kaleidoscope fragments glittered
before my eyes,
the sights, the dying sun, oranges, red,
up high on a roof, staring at the night as it bled into
the disappearing day,
the sharp sting of salt and lemon
our mouths wounded with tequila.

"I want to dance,"
Imogen said, and the next day
we joined a festival, found the parade
of carnival crowds streaming through the steaming
    streets.
Imogen basked in the sun
and danced through its shine,
I followed her flame,

watching, just in case
she tripped or fell.
She might have
burned herself
alive.

UNDERGROUND

In the crush of the tube
I watched Imogen –
her red lips pursed,
in concentration,
hair piled high
smudge of dark chocolate in the corner of her mouth
eyes on her phone.

A woman swayed, hungry-eyed
left a note beside me, on the seat –
Help me, please.

I stared at my shoes,
didn't know what to say to the pale face,
the desperate eyes,

and Imogen sighed,
then held out the bar of chocolate
and the woman went to break off a bite.

"No take it all," Imogen said, and smiled.

ON EDGE

A party with people
older than us both, but Imogen was sure
that we were welcome.

They opened their windows wide to the street
inviting the party inside,
and Imogen climbed up on to the sill,
teetering and swaying
beating time with her body,
a balancing act
as   if   she   were   about to   walk   across   a wire
that only she could see.

Of course she

                          slipped

and because I had been waiting
to   catch her
I grabbed her wrist,

and hauled her inside.

THE COST OF EVERYTHING

If you put a price on breathing,
a price on each day,
if someone asked you, what would you pay?

My dad's worth everything –
right arms, both legs,
I'd trade the lot
if it would just make him well.

Back from that trip, Imogen heard
of a treatment – a cure,
there was no question, she said,
that it would work.

It cost, mind you,

flights, accommodation
not to mention
the price of all the medication –

Mum worked a lot –
two jobs, not one –

And when we added it up,
did all the sums,
there was no way
the money was there.

So best to forget it,
don't even say it's not fair.

Dad was making his peace,
coming to terms
with the limits
of life –
observing the borders
the walls and the barriers, the no go zones.

I didn't like that acceptance,
seeing his strength diminish,
hope as concave as the flesh on his face.

"But Joe," Imogen said,
"we have to do something.
You can't sit around,
moaning and groaning."

So we washed cars
and shook buckets,
set up a crowd-funding page,
and Immie decided to put on a play.

People paid
to watch her perform,
to sing and dance and act –
and she did all of it for my dad.

GIFT

We counted the money we made:
coppers, quids,
fivers,
a tenner here and there.

People gave what they could.

We scraped down the back of the settee,
checked pockets, shook out books and bags,
called up relatives, old friends
just in case
a pot of gold might empty itself into our laps.

"Thanks, Joe, but it's no good," Mum said,
and I kicked the door,
hit a hole into the wall.

"Shit," I said, *"what now, then?"*
Immie was the one with bright ideas.

Later, she held out a fan of notes:
fifties – pink and fat.

She said it was a gift,
that it was the least she could do for Dad.

I didn't know what to say.
I knew her folks were rich –
but seriously?
This wasn't her bill to pay.

                    "Please take it, Joe," Imogen begged,
holding out that wodge of cash –

I wondered if
she'd robbed a bank,
sold a kidney, a lung –
was giving me part of herself.

GONE

Mum took Dad to the USA.

I watched Mum push him
through the airport,

Towards the miracle flight,
chasing the cure.

The space between us grew,
they shrank
into specks, ghosts, dust, then just   air.

My parents
like children
vulnerable in their hope

and I made fists of my eyes –

and Imogen held me while I cried.

US

Imogen moved in
and things changed.

We stayed up late
laughing,
cooked meals together,
messy piles of pasta,

drank beakers full of wine.
Imogen said she liked

pretending to be my   wife.

I thought about buying a ring,
I mean – I was already eighteen.

We wandered around the town

and she filled her finger
with gold and
glittering stones.

I felt proud,
but didn't know
how to pay –

I couldn't take her money again.

I applied for a credit card later that day.

CLEAN-UP

Piles of mess proliferated,
mushroomed in mouldy patches.
I dragged the hoover round,
wiped up spills and scrubbed at stains.

Imogen left her knickers on the floor,
screamed to know
where her clean clothes were.

I bumped into Dan
stayed out late –
beer, Netflix, laughing with my mate.

Imogen waited up
to tell me she'd locked me out.

I slept in Mum's car,
on the drive, in the cold.

TIRED

Imogen didn't get out of bed
and I left her there
sleeping off her mood.
When I got home from college the next day
I said,
"Why don't you just go home, then?"

She turned her body to face the wall,
her shoulders shaking,
sobs smothered by the quilt.
I walked away
not sure what else I was supposed to say.

RULES

Eat crumbs, pretend to be full –
and fix my smile the way she likes it.

Remember the right way to hold
my knife and fork

and to be silent when I swallow.

She didn't like the way I chewed,
I tried to eat quietly,
but I was confused.

She said the way I pushed my food around my plate
made her want to puke,
and she kicked me
under the table.

DISCORD

"Joe," she said,
"sometimes I don't know

what I see in you."

Later she apologized.

"I'm just tired,
and you wind me up,
sorry, Joe –
I love you,
you know.
I've proved it,
haven't I?"

I came to expect it;
that my presence was,
in essence,
disappointing.

"What did I do?"

She didn't have an answer.

I stared at my hands.
They were wide and strong, like Dad's.
My hands which could throw and hold and touch and
catch.
Gentle hands. I was a gentle lad.
I started to think there was something wrong with
that.

HORSEPLAY

Who pushed who?
Did she grab my arm and twist it before I
tickled her?
Or did she trip me first

send me flying, flattened to the floor?

In a heap we grappled laughing –
until it turned out
                    she was hurting me and I   gasped.
Hang on,
Immie,
Stop,
Please
No.
That hurts.

                    "You fucking pussy," she said.

Pain.
Not like a bellyache,
a twisted ankle,
not even like being tripped and winded,
flat on my face. No.

This was worse.
I curled up, edged away,
back against the wall –
While Immie talked. She told me
What I was.

I waited.
Because it would stop –
it always stopped,
and then there would be time for sorry and tears.

Not mine. Never mine.
Because I'm a boy and boys don't cry.

PARENTS

I was glad when Mum and Dad got back,
even though the signs weren't great
they thought we'd bought Dad
some extra days.

And I never told them where I got that cash,
they believed we'd earned it,
they never asked.

And when they asked me how I was
I didn't recognize my voice
when I said *fine*.

NOW

HERE SHE COMES

She's walking up to the witness box.

Imogen,
I almost say,
What are you doing here?

Because,

     there's no doubt that
          seeing her now,
             like this,
                    I remember

the full rhyme
of her mouth on mine,

the perfect sibilance
of her kiss,

and the couplet of our hands, joined,
the everything of that,

> not   this
> cruel history
> that tortures me –
> because it wasn't all bad,
> it couldn't have been.

I'm no poet,
but something in her
made me sing –

(Except that was a long time ago
and now is not the time
for any more extended fantasies about the past.

Because we're done
with that –)

SHE SAYS (ONE)

Oath done,
     Sworn in,
          Promise made,
               She takes the stand.

"Miss Harris,"

the barrister begins
as Imogen twists the ring
that glitters, left hand,
fourth finger
then pushes back the fringe
that's grown into her eyes –

how can she stand there and testify?

All those years
     reading messages in our palms,
          she saw the stars aligning us
               in a future that was ours.

But the stars burnt out
and so did I.

"Miss Harris,
Could you describe for the
Court, in your own words,
Your relationship
To the accused?"

There's a pause
the courtroom stalls,
and she looks up
as I look down
before she says,

"Yeah, of course.
We were together,
a couple,
best friends,"

she pauses, clears her throat,

"I guess it's a shame
that it had to end."

AMNESIA

Imogen's forgotten how it was –
or else,
it doesn't matter any more.
Years of us
dissolving here, without a thought.

But she looks sick,
sad and grim,
not smiling,
not like she's enjoying this, at least.

The barrister presses on
and I press pause
on the past –
remembering
all the things that matter
more.
Like walking free out of this court.

"And please could you tell the jury
What you were doing
On the night in question?"

I watch her expression,

but it's blank,
her eyes are small, red-rimmed,
she stands ice still,
then draws in breath
stares straight ahead
breathes out,
begins.

SHE SAYS (TWO)

"We'd been at a party —
New Year's Eve,
I didn't want to go,
I wanted to stay at home with Joe.

Just us,
nice, quiet, close —
I thought,
we were   in love, you know.

I thought he was serious
about me,
we'd been together

since we were fourteen –

God, he'd even given me a ring."

"Please answer the question,
If you can, Miss Harris.
I know this is painful for you
To revisit,
Not the sort of story
Anyone wants to have to tell
But if you could just fill us in,
On the what, the how and the when."

"No right, well, you know
I didn't have a good time.
He was flirting, and dancing,
drinking too much wine –
(he's not nice when he's drunk,
loud and lairy,
no fun,
and he scared me that night,
it was like he wanted a fight).

So I asked Joe to stop it,
and to take me home –
he'd left me standing
all on my own."

"So, you went out to the car?"

"Well, we had words,
and then
I took his keys and ran off —
I was really upset —
he'd driven us there,
and he'd driven too fast,
but I didn't complain.

I think Joe was angry,
I'd asked him to pay
back some money
earlier that day."

LIES ii

Clear
        and fast,
                her

                voice

                        is

a

        waterfall

                of

                        words
that

        feel

                rehearsed –

like she's practised telling everyone
how bad I am
so that now there's no one worse.

I know I messed up.
I know it's a mess.
I know I'm a fool –
But I can't believe she'd do this.

I keep my eyes down,   stare at my shoes,
                    bite my tongue
between my teeth   make it bleed.

HOW TO SPOT A LIAR

It's something you ought to
learn in school.

Palms will not necessarily sweat.

      (Imogen held my hand for years,
      replacing my fingerprints with hers.)

Leaping pulses do not mean lying hearts.

      (she made my heart race,
            right now it's all over the place.)

You cannot see the truth in someone's eyes.

      (if they're a window to the soul, then I guess
                some souls lie.)

THE JURY

are leaning forward
ears like cups
tipped to catch
and drink up
her story.

She tells a good tale
could make you believe the earth was flat,
that you could catch
the sun –
if you loved her enough, you'd make the effort.

I put my fingers to my face
and touch the slight indent
the ridge on my skin –
reminder of
the pound of flesh I lost
that night –

one way she's already made me pay.

SHE SAYS (THREE)

"He wasn't happy,
Joe could get like that,
moody, down –
people thought he was such a nice
    guy,
but they didn't know how hard it
    could be,

I mean, I loved him, of course I did,
but he gets sort of rough,
angry when he can't say what he
    wants –
you know he stutters,
and struggles with words –
well he didn't want to leave that
    party
with me
and go home
even though
we'd just got engaged
and like I said,
we'd had a row
about the money and
this girl, Annie Brown."

"So what happened then?"

"Well, he grabbed back the keys
and we got in the car

I was telling him to stop,
to pull up, slow down,

I was scared, I was screaming,
but he just drove faster

I knew we were heading into
disaster."

"So Mr Goodenough was driving
Dangerously, would you say?"

"Yes, of course,
he likes to go fast
he works in that garage,
he's obsessed with cars.

There are so many times
that we've nearly crashed,
I was always worried
that one day he'd smash.

And we were on
 the wrong side of the road
and I said,
Stop it, please, Joe –
You'll kill us both.

And then this car was there,
and it was too late –
we swerved, but we hit it
I remember how it felt."

She shudders and pulls
her arms tight round her chest,
she gulps, and she trembles
I sit, silent, as she says,

        "I don't remember
        what happened after that.
        It stopped and Joe
        pulled me free."

"He pulled you out of the car?"

        "Yes. He did, I think. It's hard to
         recall,

        But I could have died too,
        like that woman, poor Stephanie."

CHARACTER ASSASSINATION

Imogen's got every weapon
in her arsenal
polished and ready.

And she starts to blow up
everything I thought I was.

Like a sniper with her rifle charged,
she takes aim
and fires fast.

And I hear about,
my deliberate failure
to be any good, at anything, ever.

How I got her pregnant
and screwed up her life.
How I made her love me
and it isn't right
that I put football first
my mates, my work,
and now it's about time
I get what I deserve.

Because I let her down
over and over,
and the crash
was just another
way I proved I'm a loser.

PRESSURE

"Would you like to tell the court
In more detail,
Miss Harris,
What it was
That you and the defendant were
Arguing about that evening?"

> "Okay, sure.
> Like I said
> he owed me money.
> A lot.
>
> That made him angry
> and so
> he left me alone.
>
> He was dancing with Annie
> to make me feel bad,
> Ignoring me – it made me sad."

"How much money
Did Joseph Goodenough owe?"

> "Five thousand pounds.
> It was a loan."

CONTROL YOURSELF

My defence has a chance to try to respond
but I don't know if there's a way
to prove that Imogen's wrong.

I grind my teeth
swallow my shout –

                        control the urge
                        that's begging to howl
                        like a wolf,
                        to tear at the truth
                        and shake it
                        bloody
                        and raw
                        into this room.

The money she's on about,
she nicked it herself,
one night
from her dad
after they'd rowed.

She gave it to me
to help my dad out.
Back when I thought she actually cared.

I didn't know it was theft.

She told me about it
after Dad's trip,
after it made no difference,
when we were dealing with what that meant:

the disappointment,
despair,
as Dad's days disappeared.

She never said I had to pay her back.
I swear.

CATCH HER IF YOU CAN

My barrister looks at Imogen
like a hawk looks at a mouse,
as if she's got no hope
of escaping her claws.

She doesn't know Imogen.
I tried to warn her, but still.

Imogen's face pales and then
softens into a smile
that suggests a hint of sadness
like she just wants to help.

It's a good act.
She must have practised for hours.

She looks over at me,
so fast you'd never see,
and I hear her voice,
whispering, cruel,
"I thought you loved me —
or was that a lie too?"

"Miss Harris, do remind us
Who was driving the car?"

        Imogen speaks slowly,
        as she repeats her claim
        she sounds so certain
        so calm, but in pain:

        "Like I said,
        Joe was driving,
        I'm sorry, I'm not gonna lie

233

he was dangerous
and careless –
it's his fault she died—"

My barrister interrupts,
her calm, fair hand
steadying the court
keeping Im there on the stand.

"Miss Harris,
in your statement
to the police
you explained
that because you were drunk –"

(Im takes a tissue,
wipes her eyes,
startled, unsure,
then shakes her head)
"Yes, you, not Mr Goodenough,
as you well know –
because you were intoxicated even

– may I remind the jury
that when breathalysed on the night
in question

234

Miss Harris was found to be
well over the legal limit –

That you requested that the defendant,
drive you home
in the early hours
of the first of January."

> *"Yes, and that's the truth*
> *Joe was driving*
> *then we rowed*
> *and that's when we crashed*
> *'cos he wasn't looking*
> *at the road."*

"But, Miss Harris,
Give me a moment, if you will –
Our expert witness,
From whom the court will shortly hear,
Found your fingerprints on the steering wheel
Of that car."

> *"Yeah, I drove us to the party,*
> *Joe was teaching me to drive*
> *I've got my provisional –*
> *Is that a crime?"*

235

"I see."

My barrister turns to the judge,

"For the record, my Lord,
my client disputes this claim.
In his statement to the police
He states that he drove Imogen
To the party that night.
I wonder, Miss Harris,
If you've told other lies?

Isn't it the case, Miss Harris,
That even if you are telling the truth
To us now,
On the way to the party,
You were already drunk.
Had you not already had
Far too much?"

> *"That's a lie. No way,*
> *I'd only had one."*

"Again, my client, the accused,
As police records will sustain,
Was sober that night
And he, amongst others, disputes your claim."

236

Wouldn't you say that, given he was sober,
Joseph is a more reliable source,
Than someone who was so drunk
She could barely talk?

We have witnesses who can testify
that this was the case.
Friends of yours who can
Corroborate Joseph's claim."

                              "No, stop it.
                                  Stop lying.
                                      This isn't fair."

"Isn't it the case, Miss Harris,
That on this night –
As on so many occasions –
Your judgement was impaired,
That you were upset,
And jealous
Because your boyfriend
Was talking to a friend –
And you, being petty, wanted revenge.

So you took the keys
And ran to the car,

But he jumped in to persuade you,
To stop you breaking the law?

Isn't it the case,
That it was you at the wheel,
and you've framed your ex-boyfriend,
and that's why he's here?''

AFTER THE CRASH

CONSPIRACY

I sat,
head on my knees,
frozen,
in the rain, in the wind, in the dark.

Breathe,
someone said,
I lifted my head
and tried to see more clearly,
but everything was dark.

I took their test,
and breathed to prove
it wasn't me.

The flashing lights hurt my eyes
and I couldn't stare long

at the truth.

We waited together
for whatever
was coming.
We held hands.
She leaned into me,
and I put my arm around her,
held her tight.

Imogen was crying,
shaking,
sick,
terrified.

Pleading, and desperate,
she whispered and begged.

"You promised me, Joe,

remember what you said?"

She took my fist,
kissed it,
held it tight to her chest.

"WHO WAS DRIVING?"

the policeman said
when he came on the scene.

                                 "It wasn't me,"

Imogen replied.

                                 "It's his car,"

she explained.
"Is that right, son?"
the officer asked,
I nodded, and then it was as if someone had
cut out my tongue,
because
whatever I   said   now
was going to be   wrong.

ARREST

In custody
I handed over my phone, my keys
wallet, watch, name,
address.

The station was full of shouting,
people pissed and raging,
blokes, older than me, and dangerous.
I smelled them, felt their fury
rising and blinding –
howls of innocence and the stink of guilt
hit me,
I shook and couldn't look at the officer
who only wanted my name.

SAMPLES

Urine and blood.
Looking for evidence –
drink and drugs.

They wanted to know
how much I'd had.

Not that much.
barely anything, really.
How much is too much?
One beer? Two?
I wasn't certain I knew.

Still no chance to call my mum,
but I imagined her there,
Oh, Joe,
God, no.

MUG

Next they took my clothes,
my fingerprints,
a strand of hair.

Then a photograph –
I shivered and stared,
shit-scared –
put my hand to my face, felt the blood there –

Someone cleaned me up.
Efficient hands. Quiet voice.
"Okay, Joe, you're good to go."

Stripped back to the bone –
they knew everything about me,
all that it was possible to know
without scouring out the inside of my brain –

that would be next, I supposed.

DUTY

The solicitor looked like she'd rather be
anywhere else, but there with me.

Yawning, stale coffee breath sighs,
she flicked her eyes over some papers.
"Just say *no comment*,"
was all she'd advise.

GOTCHA

The machine beeped,
making me jump,
and I tried not to look guilty,

(but how does innocence look?
not six foot,
it doesn't stutter and shrink,
it's not hunched and crying,
it isn't weak –

it's clear, like water, like a dawn sky,
it's quiet and ready,
it's a look in the eye.)

I clenched my hands to stop the shaking,
I tried to hold the copper's stare
as he explained they'd record my words,
and checked that I understood the charge.
I pulled a blanket around me,
not faking my fear.

My solicitor looked at me,
waiting for, what?

"So, Joseph, tonight you crashed
on the B408,
and caused the death of a woman,
Stephanie White.
Can you confirm for the tape
that you were driving the car?"

I cleared my throat
and tried to find the words
that felt like truth.

"Um, yeah, me and my   girlfriend were in the car
together, coming   home."

"And you were driving?"

"Y-yeah, I said I'd   drive.
Imogen had a lot to drink."

Shit.
I said that before I'd even had time to think.

A pause –
the silence waited to be surprised
with further revelations.
I shifted in the chair,

sipped the tepid tea,
so milky and sweet
that it stuck to my teeth.

They waited a bit more,
we sat out the quiet.

**"How much did you have to drink?
What had you been drinking?"**

"J-   just a beer. Maybe two.
Not much, hours ago."
I looked up at the clock,
it was four a.m.
I yawned,
rubbed my eyes,
tried to stretch,
winced, my back ached.

"You all right, son?"

No. I'm in pain.
I didn't say that.
Didn't want to complain.

They put me back in the cell again.

CAN'T SLEEP

A cell
Is a cold place,
Cramped
Confined,
Not conducive to sleep,
But I shut my eyes.

A cell
Is a dead end,
Crying,
I still hear the calls
Of men who wanted out –
And were climbing the walls.

A cell
Is for cursed men,
For the idiots and
Fools,
For the sinners and the wicked
Who've broken the rules.

A cell
Is so lonely
It's a place with no peace.

My heart raced
And swerved
Heard a dead woman's screams.

PLEASE TELL ME

*"What   happened?
The   woman in the other car . . .
They said she was   dead –
Please tell me,   that was a   mistake."*

Morning,
but I hadn't slept,
and we were back in the blank
bare room,
and I wanted it all to be wrong.
I wanted to wake up,
pour cold water over my face,
purge the truth from my brain.

I wanted the chance to start over again.

THE VICTIM

"She had not been drinking," the officer said.
"She was not on the wrong side of the road.

The woman in the other car
was on her way home from work
after a long shift,
and
she was probably tired,
but that is not to say
she was in any way to blame."

The woman in the other car –
Mrs Stephanie White –
was a mum.

Her children,
two of them
at home,
asleep,
tucked up safe in bed,
were looking forward to seeing her
in the morning.

When she got home,

she planned to creep into their room
and kiss them quietly,
softly, so as not to disturb their dreams.
She would hug them when they woke,
listen to their love
come spilling at her,
kiss baby cheeks, and patch up toddler knees.

"Stephanie,
the woman in the other car,
had been working,
all night,

A nurse –
saving other people's lives."

WHAT HAPPENED TO HER?

Driving so fast,
she was just a blur
and
we sent her car spinning, turning, hurling
out of control.

Driving so fast,
she was caught
in that second, and there was nothing
she could do
to stop

Her car
from

SMASHING
at speed
into
the side of the road.

And there was nothing
anyone could do
to set her he   art
ticking
        again
            once
                it
                    had
                        been
                            to   rn
                                        in
                                            two.

WHAT'S THE STORY?

"Can you tell us what happened last night?
In your own words?"

No comment.

"Were you driving the car?
Your girlfriend says you were driving."

No comment.

"Your girlfriend had been drinking.
Was she the driver?"

No comment.

"What had you been drinking, Joe?
Were you even looking at the road?
Were you on your phone?
What happened last night, Joe?"

NOW

TRUTH (ii)

I almost cannot bear to watch Imogen
trying to find
a way out.

But then, sometimes the truth
has teeth
that bite
and leave a mark
and right now its jaws are fixed firmly
on her,
and she's caught
in a crocodile's jaws
sinking, pulled underwater,
drowning in the barrister's words.

And I suppose it's what she deserves.

But she's gasping, groping
as she flails,
gulps and shrieks,

> *"Stop it, stop lying,
> it wasn't me."*

"You know, Miss Harris,"
my barrister says,
"You can go through life making mistakes
But someday they'll catch up with you,
And even then, it isn't too late,
It's never too late,
To tell the truth.
Let me remind you —

You are under oath."

My barrister turns to the jury,
Almost bows,
And with a swish of her gown,
Goes to sit down.

WHO DO YOU BELIEVE?

One look at the jury
tells me not to believe
that anyone's convinced.

Sometimes it's easier to be

a girl whose tears
fall like turning leaves

Than a boy who looks tough
a boy who can't say
what he wants to in quite the right way.

I don't watch Imogen leave the stand,
she's not my concern –

I stare at the ground,
put my face in my hands.

BUT

I messed up,
I knew what she'd think, how she'd feel,–
why did I give her that ring
if I wasn't for real?

From where she was standing
it looked like betrayal
that I'd lied to her, didn't love her –
it's true – I did fail.

Pathetic,
I was;
Fact –   I still am.

I didn't make it clear
that I was done.

Because when someone needs love
and then you take it away –
but I didn't want her to say
that we were engaged.

My stomach curdles, fists curl,
chest aches,
it's my fault.

And, God, I'm so sorry –
for all of this hurt.

PART THREE

NOW

COURT ADJOURNED

I'm allowed to go home,
and breathe in what's left of the day,
free air,
shadows and sunlight and traffic and somewhere
over there
people laughing.

What comes next –

                        tomorrow?

What about the day after that, and the next?
My footsteps beat out questions on the
indifferent street.
I don't know if today
has been enough,
if tomorrow I will be able to say
the words I must,
and slip through this net, or
if there will be a new chain around my neck.

Did they believe that
Imogen's truth is my lie?

Avoiding all the shouts
the stares and flashing lights
the press who want my guts
spilled all over their pages
we hurry,
Mum's hand in mine,
as if we're running away from a crime.

TELLY ON

Phone off
we block out the world
and wait for the nurse.

Here, at home, other things matter,
like breathing easier for a while.

MEDICINE

The district nurse calls,
later than usual.

Dad's in his chair, patient,
waiting.

Skin like tissue paper
webs of veins,
dark with pain, needing
the relief of her needle.

Soft,
faded,
my dad's hand is bruised and sore,
once tough and tan –
callouses making me shriek
as firm fingers tickled
the soft undersides of my squirming arms,
dirt under his nails
from hard, honest work,
face tired but eyes full of love,
for me,

his boy.

He called me Joey first,
his baby Joey
always carried, no pouch –
but up high, tall, in arms, on his back,

legs dangling round his head:
I was king surveying all.

Now on bad days, I carry him,
supporting his weight
being careful to be gentle,
but my hands still causing pain.
Bones moving,
then his sharp inhale.
And I share his agony, in a way.

We shuffle
where once we ran,
we pause, to rest
after steps, not miles –
bent over, chest heaving
not from laughing.
Wan smile
is all we have –
eyes not meeting, too awful to see.

I don't want to give him anything else
to carry,
wish I could shoulder this
on my own.

"Let's get this straight,"
Dad said, the day I told him –
leaning forward, his eyes slits.
"You're planning on going to prison
for a crime you didn't commit,
you're planning on letting Imogen
get away with this?
Please tell me, son,
you're not that thick."

The room was boiling hot,
(heating turned right up
because he was always cold)
stifling, I couldn't breathe –
my dad grabbed my hand, said,
"Joe, come on, get real."

I can't stay in,
and, even though I shouldn't,
I leave the house
and all that other pain
for them to deal with on their own.

TAKE ON THE DARKNESS

I wander down to the park,
skirt the groups of kids
and sink into the shadows,
and make the mistake
of turning on my phone.

It lights up

and Imogen's messages leap out
to get me by the throat.

> *help me,*
> > *you bastard –*
> *I'll finish you*
> > *I need you.*

> *please, help me*
> > *I'll die.*

> *call me.*

> > *I love you.*

THEN – AFTER THE CRASH

POLICE BAIL

Curfew set at six p.m,
not allowed to contact Imogen –
passport handed in –
I was stuck.

Because I always tried
to do the right thing –
I was fucked.

Imogen didn't pick up her phone,
and although Mum told me not to call,
not to bother her, or make a scene,
I took Mum's phone and dialled her number,
as we rode the bus home.

HOME

I wanted to disappear upstairs
to my room –
wash off the cell,

and the death
and the fear
and the lies
and sleep my way back into
being a child.

But Dad was there,
in the hall,
leaning heavily on his stick,
up and out of his chair,
his breathing slow, thick.
I wanted to tell him to go,
to sit back down
and leave me alone.
I didn't want to try to explain
what I'd done.

"Hell, lad, what the hell's gone on?" he said.
"What happened last night?
Tell me, Joe, you weren't driving drunk?"
I shook my head, then whispered, "*No.*"
"There's that then, but bloody hell.
This could ruin your life, you know."

I walked up to my room, and slammed the door,
couldn't bear to see their faces any more.

DOORSTEP

I wasn't supposed to contact her,
but there was no way
not to.

No one answered
as I beat a fury on her front door.

"Immie," I yelled, *"Immie, it's me."*
Dark windows laughed
And I scooped a fistful of gravel and threw it – hard.

WHERE THERE'S A WILL

Imogen's best mate, Kiran,
who was seeing my friend Dan,
told Dan who told me,
where to find her.
Easy.

I caught the bus to the hospital,
tried not to think about the night before,

just about
putting things right,
although that was not something
anyone could arrange.
It wasn't a question
of reshuffling the cards,
of laying out a new hand
then playing a fairer game.

I was hemmed in,
caught,
couldn't reverse.

It was New Year's day.
I should have been with the lads,
celebrating victory
after the match
or going to my nan's
for a slap-up tea,
falling asleep on the sofa,
warm inside full-belly dreams.

I jumped off a stop early,
needing to walk,
to try to breathe
past houses and gardens

where no one knew me.

But the white skies stared,
glassy with rain.
And the world was looking at me,
the streets knew my name.

Blame boggled,
wide-eyed
from the windows
in town
like it blazed on my chest –
the truth of this crime.

HOSPITAL

The sting of antiseptic air
scored my nostrils,
scraped the back of my throat.
Walking down corridors
that wound on for ever,
I was lost
in a maze –
I'd never get out.

Criminal creeping,
I jumped,
and dodged,

as my trainers squeaked,
giving away who I was.

WARD D2

You had to press a button to get in.
I said I'd come to see Imogen Harris,
and they asked my name.

I lied.
Said, *It's Stefan. Stefan Harris. Imogen's brother.*
There was a pause.

And then the door opened when I pushed.

Stefan happened to be away,
skiing somewhere with his mates,
but they didn't know that, did they?

INVISIBILITY

Imogen was half sitting up in bed,
her arm in a sling
and her ankle bandaged.
She looked pale
fake tan faded,
her skin a queasy yellow.
But she was wearing her favourite hoodie,
that ring glittering in the light,
a cup of tea on the stand by her bed.
She was staring at her phone,
and nobody was bothering her.

She didn't notice me at first
and I stood there for a while,
waiting,
for her to see me,
thinking
maybe I'd been disappearing
piece by
      piece by
               piece.

AHEM

I coughed.

She looked up,
and leaned up,
sort of screamed,

> "Shit, Joe, you scared me,
> What are you doing here?
> I mean ..."

"I wanted to see how you are.
Check everything was okay.
You didn't pick up,
Didn't answer my messages
So I was worried."
I swallowed, forced it out,
"Weren't you bothered about me?"

> "Oh my God, of course I was,
> Joey, come here."

She held out her arm, the one that was free,
I stayed where I was,
leaning against the end of the bed
I needed it to hold me up.

She started to explain,

> "But look at me, look at the state
>   of me.
> My ankle's sprained, it hurts so
>   much.
> And my wrist.
> I couldn't talk, not with the
>   doctors
> and police
> and everything
> and my dad's on his way."

FAULT

I didn't tell her I'd been locked up all night.
Instead I said,

"The woman in the other car,
you know,
that woman died."

Imogen covered her mouth with her hand,
although surely she must have realized.

"They breathalysed me, Joe,
so, you know . . .
don't ask me to . . .
I really can't . . .
Please.
I feel like hell,
stuffed with tubes,
look at me,
oh, God, no, no, no."

I said it,
quietly,
but I'm not sure she heard,
because she was so loud –

*"Imogen, please,
what are we going to do?"*

IMOGEN'S PLAN

"What did you say to the
    police?
What did you tell them?"

"Nothing," I said.
"No comment."
I didn't tell her
I'd said I'd been driving,
or that
I'd told them she was pissed,
or that I thought maybe it had all gone wrong
long before this.
Her body loosened,
a smile inched into her cheeks
and she reached out to me again.

                              "Okay, thanks, babe,"
                              Imogen said.
                              "That's such a relief,
                              I don't think you'll get long
                              if they get you at all –
                              I mean, you were sober, right?
                              Not like me.
                              It'll just be careless driving,
                              don't you agree?"

"What are you talking about?"

Her voice fell,
face paling,
she spoke furiously,

words tight with intent,
splitting with fear –

> "Just say it was an accident, right,
> that the car skidded in the rain,
> tell them whatever,
> just don't mention my name.
> I'm sure you'll
> sort it out.
> Because I already
> made my statement,
> I already said, without a doubt
> that I wasn't the driver,
> Joe, come on."
> She covered her ears,
> whimpered,
> "Please, don't shout."

NOW

DOG

Once she whistled
and I crawled
on my belly

licking for scraps,
panting for pats.

She thinks I'll come running
again.

Time to stand up,
Time to grow up
Walk tall.

I turn off my phone,
turn around,
go home.

WORDS

Not sure when silence became easier
than trying to be heard.
She bit   my words in half.

I chewed and stewed   the truth
for months:
didn't dare to say it aloud.

MAXIMUM SENTENCE

is fourteen years.

I try to see that time in my head,
older Joes
                                    future selves.

People say
I look like my dad,
and I stare at photos
of my folks –
they married young:
here's Dad at twenty-one.

Will I be as strong?
Or be as happy
as he was back then –
look at him,
holding my mum's hand.

In three more years,
I'll be the same age,
and I don't want to think about
how prison could change
who I planned to become.

DAD

isn't getting better
but we
can't complain
because the fact he's still alive
is something of a miracle,
Mum says.

She goes to mass every Sunday
and gets down on her knees
and I know
that I should join her,
even though I don't believe.
"But they gave him two years, Joe,
he's already done so well –
what if he beats this?
I've got a feeling he might,
you know."

I'm glad it's dark
so I can't see her face
and the hope in her eyes
that we both know is lies.
The movie flickers
on the TV

and I try to watch,
banish the ifs and the buts
and the coulds and the maybes,
I wish I could deal in certainty.

"If you get off these charges, Joe,"
Mum says,
"I swear we'll go away.
I'll get the money somehow
and we'll have a proper holiday."

I take her hand,
like I'm a little kid again.

THEN – AFTER THE CRASH

NEGOTIATIONS

We got a call a week later,
a summons
to the station.

Felt sick, sitting there, waiting.

Mum beside me, messing with her bag,
pulling out
handfuls of receipts,
searching in its depths
for something to distract –
she'd have climbed in there if she could.

She found a pack of mints,
held it out,
her hands shaking
and I wanted to hold on to her
and tell her it would be okay,
that we'd be all right,
but I didn't dare tell
any more lies.

Finally I was called.
Death by Dangerous Driving
the charge sheet read.
I nodded, accepting
what it said.

Mum held herself upright
face pinched with fear,
like the time when we waited
for Dad to get the all clear,

We sat down
and she put her head
between her knees.

My hand on her back
I felt her shoulder blades
slice through her coat
and saw my mum shrinking
with every extra load
that added to the weight.
"Sorry, Joe,"
she croaked.
"It's just
It's hit home –
I don't know
What I'll do?
Oh hell,
what now, Joe?"

COWARD

It comes from the Old French –
means an animal

with its tail between its legs.

And that was me,
a miserable dog,
slinking, shrunk, half-sized,
waiting to be kicked up the backside.

BREAKING BAIL

I had to see Imogen.
I couldn't go on –
I'd charged my old phone,
got a new sim,
she'd been calling, texting
she wanted me to write it in blood:

A promise to exchange
My life for her lies.

I met her at the park.
We shivered together on the swings
side by side,
the chains rattled and clashed,

and I kicked at the ground.

> "Joe, please,
> stop messing me around,
> what are you going to say?
> Are you going
> to take the blame?"

She put her hand into mine.

"I'm sorry about this."
I was about to let her down.

> "Wait, Joe,
> you do still
> love me, right?"

Time stretched, seconds gaped
like hours,
and then,
"Course I do,"
I lied.

> "So, let's do something nice,
>
> let's go back to mine."

She pulled me up and off the swings
and through the park.
It was getting dark
and she moved up close
to steal m**y** warmth,
filled my pockets with her hands.

No one was there
at Imogen's house.

We lay beside each other in her bed
naked.
I couldn't get hard
but she didn't laugh.

She held up her phone,
and took a picture of us
and sent it straight through to me.

"Keep that, always,
you're my person," she said.
"If I didn't have you,
I don't know who I'd be."

BUT

Her love was wearing thin
like paper,
I could rip it into shreds,
put it into my mouth
and churn it into pulp,
spit out grey mush –

Whatever it was she said,
whatever words she used,
it couldn't make us real again –

there was nothing left.

EVIDENCE

I got home,
fists still screwed up tight
in memory
of the night
a woman died.

I made Dad a tea
and ran upstairs
because
I needed to be prepared
to show the world I was not guilty.

I held up my phone
and stared at the picture that would prove
I wasn't the driver.

Our seatbelts had left us both marked –

and the mark on me was
across my heart –

a bruise that no one had asked to see.

PROOF

I sent Imogen a text
and sat
twitching in my room,
waiting for a reply.

The photograph was proof
that she couldn't deny.

Finally she answered,
like nothing had changed,
like this was all a good game.

> *what are you saying, Joe?*
> *want to come over,*
> *say it to my face?*

I read her response, then typed
fast,
teeth in my lips
trying not to bite.

-shut up, Imogen, please
this isn't a joke-

> *I mean it, babe, come over*
> *i'm still horny.*

-Imogen, I swear,
we have to go to the police.-

> *oh no we don't.*
> *it isn't proof.*

-let's see what my lawyer thinks.-

what? are you threatening me?

-I don't think so, no.-

it doesn't really feel that way

-I can't lie in court
why won't you
just tell the truth?-

i don't know what you mean

-you do-

screw you

CAN'T SLEEP

Rattle of stone on glass –
I lay in bed
refusing to get up,
to even lift my head.

I told myself it was the wind.

289

The rain.
My imagination.
A ghost.

I shut my eyes and spun
back into the past,
holding my pillow, grabbing at the sheets,
gritting my teeth
against
the blood
and death.

SURPRISE

Next morning, first thing,
Imogen was
at my house, on the step.
Thank God Mum was at work
and Dad was asleep.
They'd told me not to see her,
not to break bail again.

She stood there, waiting,

crumpled, like she hadn't slept,
like she was sickening for something
like I was causing that pain.

"What are you doing here?"

                                    "Can we talk?" she begged.

She followed me upstairs,
finger looped into my jeans
and then we sat on my bed

not touching.

I slid to the floor
so I couldn't see her face,
leant my back against the wall
and waited

for whatever she'd come to say.

She began,

                        "So, you're going to tell them?"
"If I have to, if you won't."
                        "But Joe—"
"No, listen,

I can't do this to my folks."

            "Joe, I'll go to prison."

"You won't, you're seventeen."

            "So, you've thought it through
                then?"

"Of course—"

            "Don't be so fucking mean."

*"Imogen, it's not as if
I'm doing this to hurt you."*

            "So what then, Joe?
            You just want to ruin my life?
            I'd rather die."

"Don't."

            "Don't what? Don't tell the truth?"

*"It isn't fair.
Just face it,
It was you."*

            "You bastard."

*"No I'm not,
I've loved you,
Immie, so long.
But now—"*

            "Yeah, what?"

*"You're kind of
On your own."*

PAIN

I'd just finished us
again –
properly, no games.

I couldn't look at her,
couldn't find a way
to meet her eye,
instead I said,

"I have to think about me for a change,
my mum and dad
my future, my life.
I don't want a criminal record,
I don't want to tell these lies.
It was good for a bit,
but we're done.

Imogen, remember how it used to be?
Well, I think that's all gone."

But when I looked at her
I saw her pain, her eyes bleeding
tears again.
*"Well, I guess I'll **have to get over it**,"*
she threw my words
back in my face.

KNOCK, KNOCK

It was late for visitors – I looked at Mum,
she paused the film and went to answer the door.

Imogen's dad was on the step and
his car was parked out front, wheels up on the kerb,
so close to the house, like he was scared he'd be
   robbed.
A shadow was hunched in the seat
in the back
and my heart lurched with the thought
of what that meant.

Mr Harris clicked the fob, locked the car,
and he nodded, didn't wait to be invited inside
just shouldered in, as if that was fine.

He filled up the space, with his voice, with his height,
and Mum drew herself up, ready to fight.

"How can we help?
Should you even be here?"

                Mr Harris wasn't daunted,
                he nodded, and spoke,

"I've come to suggest something,
So just give me a minute –
This problem we've got,
With your Joe and my girl,
It's a mess, I know,
But I want you to think.
I've got a suggestion,
Perhaps it will appeal,
If Joe pleads guilty,
We could do a deal."

"A deal?"
Mum's voice tore into the space
and he stepped back,
like she'd spat in his face.
Dad started to stir.
opened his eyes,
stared at our visitor.

"A deal?" he sighed.

"Good evening," Mr Harris said
  to my dad,
And he offered a handshake
that wasn't returned.
"I'm sorry to see you

Still so sick,
And I'm sure some money
Could help out with bills –
It can't be easy
Living like this.
If Joe goes to prison how will you
    cope?
Perhaps you'll allow me to offer
    my help
In return for Joe changing his plea
Making it clear that he will,
of course,

               plead guilty."

"Joe's not going anywhere," Mum laughed in his face.
"And I can't believe you've come here –
you should be ashamed.
It's no wonder your daughter
has turned out this way.
Maybe if you tried
to bring Imogen up
to know the difference
between right and wrong
we wouldn't be in this mess.
My Joe's done nothing
he just tried his best."

Harris narrowed his eyes, and looked at my mum
as if she was something unpleasant,
insignificant scum –
I knew what he was thinking,
before he opened his mouth,
that he was disgusted his daughter
ever set foot in our house.

"Your son's a disgrace,
he's used my girl.
He's a waste of space.
And now she's hurt.
He's broken her heart,
she doesn't sleep,
she'll fail her exams,
she won't eat.
Her future's in bits,
He doesn't care.
People like you
have got no idea
of what decency means.
You're scum, d'you hear."

"Get out," Mum yelled,
her face up close to his.
"Get out of our home.

You piece of shit."

Harris was pale,
eyes dark, full face of stubble,
he swore back, foul-mouthed,
then rooted in a pocket,
a desperate man
who wouldn't leave us alone
couldn't give up this chance to force his point home.
But before he could speak or say anything more,
Imogen was there, in the shadow of the hall.
"Dad, come on, let's go,
forget it,
there's no point
any more."

"We'll see you in court,"
Mum hurled at their backs.
"Make sure you
shut the door
on your way out."

NOW

BIRD SONG

Alarm sharp
it snaps me out of sleep,
spring's urgent call.

I know
what I've got to do:

stay true,
sing my own tune.

I barely slept
last night –
and when I did
it was only to dream
of Stephanie.

I guess I'll never stop
being guilty.

EARLY

Lying on my bed
the sun slips through the blinds
and I hear a noise
that softly breaks the news
that I am not alone.

Mum's radio plays cheerful songs
and voices,
hers and Nan's,
are an answer
to the question of why
it's worth it to be brave.

The doorbell goes and I hear the
sound of friends,
Annie and Dan,
who are sticking around,
who know who I am.

I stretch, yawn,
put a hand on my chest
to slow my heart beat
before the final test.

GOODBYES

I try not to imagine
not coming home.

Yesterday I stood in my bedroom
and tried not to cry.
Now I fix my hair
and straighten my tie.

I stand here
looking at my stuff:
desk piled high
with books and files,
the university letter confirming my place,
the stacks of notes, the effort I've made
for a future that might not be mine.

A photo of me and my folks,
ones of me and Annie and Dan –
my team, the lads,
the good stuff, none of the bad.

I pull on my clothes,
feel grateful for
stuff I've learned to notice:

soft towels,
nice clothes,
a clean bed.
I turn off my phone –
can't bear to see her messages any more.

ANNIE

I told her not to come over
but here she is
in the kitchen with Mum
making tea,
bacon sarnies,
and smiling
acting like this is just another day.

I get it,
understand the sentiment,
that she's trying to help.

Only, it's not fair.

We stand in the garden

I stare at the clear sky –
summer's almost here this morning
breathing warmly on our skin.

And then
I say,
"Look, Annie, you know,
if I get sent down
don't worry about me, I'll be fine."

She smiles at me and shakes her head,
"That's not even happening,
you can't think that way.
Joe, everyone's expecting you
to come home today,
we believe in you, right?
So shut up, okay?"

FRIENDS

Dan bursts out of the back door,
heads the ball across the yard, and I knock it back.

Annie's watching,
then tackles Dan when he's not looking
sends him sprawling,
and then we're laughing
as she holds out a hand to pull him up.

Annie cares about what's right.

I like Annie Brown
and she likes me.
If only everything
could be so easy.

I reach for my phone,
turn it back on
see another message
that I'll have to erase.

Joey, let's forget yesterday
forget what went down,
I know I can trust you
with everything right?
Like – everything – like – my life.
I know you won't hurt me, not in the end
And maybe after all this, we'll still be friends?

I hold the screen up to my friends
and cover my eyes
so I can't see their faces,
or hear them spit fire.

"This is out of order, Joe.
It's against the law,
you need to report her,
you've got to make sure
that no one believes her,
that no one in that court
thinks a word that she says
is worth a thing,
bloody hell, you should have her arrested
it's emotional blackmail, can't you see?"

I know it's right
I know they're on my side,
I know what I have to do

it's going to be soon.

TRUST

"Do you trust me?" Imogen said, way back then,
on the ice – first date –
when she held my hand,
I was wobbling
finding my feet,
never even dreaming this.

Even then I knew
that my answer mattered.
I wondered,
would she watch me fall?
Drop into the suffocating cold
and let it feather me frozen,
feed on my warmth?

I think I always knew
that no one
was really
one hundred per cent
true.

But I laughed and told her,
"Yes, of course I trust you,
of course I do."

BACK IN COURT

I guess if it were me,
I'd read those stories
the newspapers print,
and believe
that I was guilty too,
that trying to shift the blame
is the coward's thing to do.

They'll report on my looks, my cheap suit,
on my mum and my dad,
they'll say that it's fact –
I was born bad.

But I face them all down,
the reporters, the crowd,
I know the truth
got to speak it, loud.

It's time for my defence
to get the unsayable said.
It's time to make a difference,
change that jury's mind,

let in light and
pull the curtains wide.

307

FIRST WITNESS FOR THE DEFENCE

DANNY

"Mr Gill,
How long have you known the accused,
Mr Goodenough?"

My barrister smiles, encouragingly
Danny is red and uncomfortable
strangled by his shirt and tie.

"Long enough to know
that he's a good bloke."

"Yes?" My barrister nods him on.

"I mean,
he's been my mate since we were kids
we played for the same team,
hung out, done everything
together for years."

"But when did that change?
How did you feel
When Imogen Harris came onto the scene?"

"Um, at first it was fine
she was okay I guess –

and then it changed,
Joe came out less and less.

It was like when Imogen said jump,
he said how high.
When I asked him what's up
he would lie, say he's fine.

We knew it was dodgy
when he gave up the team
because football's his life
he's amazing.

It just wasn't like him
not to show up,
to avoid his mates
just 'cos he was 'in love'."

Dan makes quotes with his fingers,
and rolls his eyes,
like this love thing's a joke,
a big pack of lies.
Since he split up with Kiran

he's changed,
he's more cynical and angry –
he says girls are insane.

He folds his arms,
stares my barrister down,
she smiles,
says, "Thank you, do carry on."

Dan finishes off,
"Yeah well, I guess Joe changed."

"Excuse me your honour" –
the prosecution intervene –
"Is this witness relevant?
does the court really need to hear
the ins and outs of this nonsense,
this is a court – can we please make that clear?"

The jury snigger
and I try not to doubt,
but my shoulders ache
with the effort of
sitting up straight.

But it's true,

sometimes Imogen wanted me to stick close.
My mates took the piss.

Immie's bitch,
Joey's whipped.

I never knew,
when too much was not enough,
or when too little was too much.

My barrister continues,
breezy and blithe,
she cuts to the chase
and brings out her knives.

"The point is, Mr Gill,
Could you please tell the court
If Joseph would
Take the blame for a crime
He did not commit
If his girlfriend
Miss Harris,
Insisted he did?"

"Totally
yeah, it was sad, I guess

311

but Joe changed,
he did whatever she said.
It's like she had this weird hold and
Joe wasn't the same,
if he loved her, whatever,
he still shouldn't have taken the blame.
But Imogen was toxic
a pathological liar,
all the lads thought that –
but Joe, he was blind,

he went mad when I told him
that he needed to watch out."

TRUTH (iii)

I don't think the jury buy
a single word Dan's said,
they know he's my best mate,
and the way he's talking about Imogen
isn't quite right –
and I don't like it.

It wasn't all her fault.
I was just as bad.

Then the barrister presses on
with a smile.

"Kiran Sawar your ex-girlfriend
Told this court
She watched Joseph Goodenough
Drive away from the party
At your house that night.

Mr Gill, can you tell this court please
Is this the truth?
Is this right?"

"No. It's a lie.
Kiran was with me.
We were upstairs
in my bedroom at the back.
There's no way she could have seen,
she's talking crap."

Dan's looking strong
defence is his thing
and he's all over it now,

arguing, leaning in
to take that ball,
boot it into the stands,
protect the goal,
to the cheers of the fans.

But the prosecution insist
that someone's got to be lying.
Can he prove what he says?
They think they've got him
without even trying.

"No way." Dan's loud
defiant, mad.

                    "So your girlfriend is a liar?
                    She's made all this up?"

"Well, yeah. She's my ex.
It's bollocks, mate.
They're both off their heads.
Don't believe what she said."

TEXTS

The jury are shown evidence
that makes me shrink
into my seat,
I can't bear the weakness
they're going to see.

Imogen, please,
I don't want to lie.

> *What lies?*
> *Come on, Joe,*
> *You're a big boy*
> *Man up, do the time.*

No, I can't go to prison.

> *You'll be fine.*

Please, Imogen,
don't make me do this,
don't make me
say it was you.

> *No one will believe you,*
> *Joe, even if you do.*

But I'm scared,

> *God, you're weak,*

And my dad,

　　　　　　　　He'll be all right,

And my life.

　　　　　　　　You'll get out.

I can't.

　　　　　　　　You can.

"Inadmissable evidence,"
the prosecution sound bored,
these messages prove nothing
except I'm running scared.

TOXICOLOGY REPORT

It clears me –

　　　　　　　　　　of something,

proves to the jury that
I wasn't drunk that night,
I'm not all bad,
I didn't drink and drive.

But I still took that car,
because I wanted to look good,
and I lied to the police,

I didn't tell the truth.

I let Imogen down
when I didn't fix her pain.
I made this mess
I deserve some blame.

MY TURN

Sworn in,
I stand waiting.
Legs shaking.

The judge's face is lined
and old,
as if he's seen and heard it all
a hundred times before
and I'm just another fool he'll have to send to jail.

IF ONLY

I could start again.

I wish I'd never noticed her,
never held her hand.
Wish I'd never kissed her,
loved her,
missed her.
If only I'd never reached out – glued myself
sticky fingered, tight to that girl.
She'd have been better off without me,
there'd have been no strife.
We'd have grown up less screwed up,
we'd be living our lives.

WHAT DO YOU PLEAD?

I draw breath,
and stand tall, shoulders back.

I do it,
I look them in the eye,

The woman with the dyed red hair,
A bloke whose tie is the colour of my team,
Another whose face is so stern I can't breathe,
The lad who's leaning forward, eyes fixed on me,
The old lady wearing specs, disapproving and grim.
The hipster,
The goth,
The granny,
The priest,
The man with the specs and the massive grey beard,
The woman who's pregnant, eyes full of tears.
The row of people who hold my life in their hands,
All twelve of them.

I look them in the eye,
And I say
Clearing my throat,
Coughing and then
Clear as a bell

"I'M   NOT   GUILTY."

(so why do I still feel guilty as hell?)

ANOTHER WAY

I force myself to look up
at Stephanie's family.

"I'm sorry," I say –
pretending there's no one else here,
I try to make it sound bigger
try to make them hear
and before a single question is asked,
I get it out there.
"I - I - I mean it,
I'm sorry.
I want you to know
That what happened,
It was   terrible…
I never   wanted   things to go—"

"Mr Goodenough," the judge shouts me down.
"Silence, be quiet,
you must abide
by the rules of this court."

I swear I won't pretend
that Stephanie didn't matter –
I'm not proud of my part,

and her family deserve better.

My barrister's face tells me
I can't mess up again.

"Can you tell us what happened,
in your own words,
everything you know
take your time, Joe,
be as clear as you can
don't leave anything out,
remember, now – everything counts."

MY STORY i

MY STORY ii

"My parents were away,
They'd travelled abroad
my d-dad wasn't w-well –
we thought it might h-help."

(watched them leave
Mum so small
Dad waving, thumbs up
acting like all
would be well.)

I swallow   breathe
Take my   time
Even though I sound stupid,
Even though I sound slow.
But the clock's ticking,
And I'm not doing well.

(look at that guy
in his wig, his gown,
like he's on starter's
orders,
he wants to take me
down.

Sob story, *he'll yell* –
Irrelevant
Enough
I stumble on
before he can make me
stop.)

"Imogen stayed with me
whilst they were gone,
but when they came back,
she had to go home."

("Let me stay, Joe,"
she said,
"please,
I don't want
to go –
come with me,"
she begged.
        "I can't
        be on my
                        own.")

(Turned my back
            on her –
thinking about Dad,

I was fraying,
        like thread,
stretched, taut
        about to snap.)

"So it was hard then,
And we weren't getting on,
I wanted to do better but
Im was on one."

                    (I drove her home

carried her stuff
inside her house, it was
empty, dark,
smelled bad, like
something

                    had died.
No one was in,
and I fed the cat,
turned on the heating,
made her a brew,
tried to act
like this was all right,
then I went home.)

"'On one?' Joseph, please
Can you explain?"

"It felt like it was too much.
There was a lot going on.
With school and my job,
trying to be a good son.
And Im didn't get it,

                    (she texted at night
                    called me at work,
                    then didn't show up

when she's promised
she would.)

I tried to make it work
Told her she was still
   welcome,
Mum had done a roast,
Dad was up,
Out of bed,
Nan had come over,
To celebrate
I'd heard about my place
At uni that day."

(I watched the clock –
half past nine
I was just washing up,
house so still and quiet,
I looked up, through the
window,
to stare at the stars,
she was there,
sitting out
on the step,
head in her hands.

I look at the jury,
want to see they're
    impressed.
see if they get
that I'm not what they
    guessed.

"You're late," I said,
shivering my news,
into the dark,

she shrugged,
got up,
turned around
walked off.)

My barrister tries to get
    me to
get to the point –
"So Joseph,
Your relationship
Was in trouble?"

"Yeah – I mean
I think we'd come to the
    end,

326

different stuff going on –
we were growing apart –
it was Christmas,
she went to her dad's –
she asked me to go with
    her,
but I couldn't you know –
might have been my dad's
    last."

(opening presents
seeing Dad
smile at mine.
a photo of us
ten years ago
blown up
full size
me in my kit,
muddy knees
gappy smile
perched on Dad's
shoulders
him holding me
                    high.)

I pause again,

search the face of my
    brief
who nods at me to
    continue,
to make the jury see.

LAST DATE i   ## LAST DATE ii

"The day before
    New Year's
we had a date.
I wanted to talk,
sort everything out.

                              (Stupid
                              I was,
                              thinking we'd change
                              but I thought I still loved
                                  her,
                              I didn't want the pain
                              of letting it go
                              though even Dad said,
                              "Just call it a day, son,

time to move on,
time to think of your future,
you're much too young,
to tie yourself down, Joe,
just give it a rest.")

It didn't work."

(Romantic meal for two,
eating garlic bread
on my own
at the Italian in town –
in my smart shoes
I'd stressed over my hair,
stank of aftershave,
sat at the table,
sweating and checking my
    phone.)

"She didn't show up?"

(Maybe something had
    happened,
something bad,
that could be it,
I shifted on my chair,
didn't know if I should look
    for her,
or wait, or just text again.)

"Well, yeah, she was late,
we had another fight.
Basically it was over
that's what I thought,
after that night."

(*Lipstick smeared*
like she'd been kissing
someone else,
eyes shot red,
she laughed at me
when I told her she was
late,
"Poor baby,"
she said, voice kind of snide.
"Fuck you, fuck this," I said,
making her cry.)

(*I put my gift, the ring*
she'd asked for,
on the table
and left.
Why couldn't I care,
just a little bit less?)

RING

With this ring
I thee   –   what?

Not love.
Maybe hate's more what it was.

It was getting hard to find the difference
between those extremes.

Why did I leave it there?
I could have kept it secret and safe
in my pocket,
returned it to the shop
then cut up the credit card
and made a clean break.

But I put it on the table
a symbol of my   disgust.

Discarded diamonds
angry gold, a twist of what we'd lost.

NEW YEAR'S EVE   NEW YEAR'S EVE ii

"But then on New Year's
Eve she said she was sorry

(She texted,

I love you

and

it made me cry)

I went over to sort it
get it right, be a man.

(She was

excited

But when I got there,
  she said,

'Oh, Joe, you're amazing,
you got me the ring,

had the ring on her finger

wouldn't

listen to

me.)

it's beautiful, babe,
does this mean what I think?'

I paused.
Tried to think of the best thing to say,
then I stepped back, told her,
'No, that's not what I meant.'

> (She didn't hear,
>   she was dancing,
>
> full of laughter, wound tight,
>   holding me,
> kissing me,
>   not wanting to fight.
>
> I know all her songs,
>   I've learnt all her lines,
> I'm part of the beat,
>   part of the rhymes,
> I'm hers, off by heart –
>
> and I still
>   don't know
> where I end
>   where she starts,
> I'm still,
>   bound too close,
> we're   knotted and tied

can't sever the threads

    that strangle me silent,

whatever she says.)

I wanted to talk,
to sort everything out,
but she wasn't listening,
there was no chance."

(I lay back, gave up,
swallowed by
her cushions,
    a throw,
teddies, and headphones,
stuff strewn, in a mess
possessions,
      stuff,
I was just something else.

"I missed you," she said,

and that hurt,
the most.)

FIGHT

FIGHT ii

"Can you please take us
    through
The events of that night.
Don't worry, Joseph,
Take your time."

Maybe I seem
nervous, on edge –
my barrister speaks softly,
like she's keeping me calm
she doesn't want me to
    blow
what we've done up to
    now,
I know I've got to focus –
but I don't know how.

"We went to the party,
I   thought it would
    be fine –
we'd stay for a bit, and
    then I'd go home.
And somehow I'd
    sort   this

make her get that we
were done."

*(I was talking to Annie,
laughing with Dan,
but Imogen wanted to tell
    everyone
the plan,
waving her hand around
showing off the frigging ring
flashing a sign
that it was happening –*

Joe and Immie Forever

but it was a lie.

*"No, Imogen, listen,
that's not what I meant,"
Her arms were around me,
tight at my neck:*

*"What the fuck?" she
    whispered
her teeth in my cheek,
"You don't mean that Joe,*

336

you owe me, don't you
think?")

"Yeah well, we got to
    Dan's party
then it all blew up,
it was nasty, we were angry,
and she bit my face
I was standing there,
    bleeding
in front of my mates.
I felt like an idiot,
I looked a fool,
and I didn't know what else
    I could do.
It couldn't go on,
all the fighting and the pain

I didn't know how to stop
    it,

didn't know what else I
    could say.

                (she hung on
                        me
                                hands
                grabbing at my throat

337

I choked
she twisted,
            gripped
pulled something tight
                it ripped –
the necklace
            she'd given me,

        that I always wore –

        on the carpet
                in bits.)

She took my keys,
then she ran,
but I followed her –
legged it out into the street.

I jumped in the car
told her to stop,
'Please. Pull over,
slow down,' I begged."

                (foot down,

                    speeding
                slammed back
in my seat,
        she ran a red light
I started to scream.)

("Imogen, please,
you're going too fast,
Immie, stop,
come on,
you're drunk."

Out of the town and
into the dark,
a darkness so thick
it swallowed us up,
no streetlights,
no moon,
not a sliver,
a slice,
to light up the road,
and make it easy to drive —)

I hold onto the box
I'm shaking now,
leg jumping, dry-mouthed,
sweat on my lip
and on my brow.

"Joe, are you all right?
Can you carry on?"

("Joe, I hate you,"
she screamed)

"Yeah, well
it was raining and dark and
the wipers were bust,
Imogen couldn't see
where she was going
it happened so fast.

> (*not looking at the road*
> *looking at me*
> *firing bullets of pain*
>
> *"I don't care if we die,"*
> *and it hit me –*
> *again*
> *slap*
> *bang*
> *there*
> *in the heart:*
> *what I'd done.*)

That night I'd watched her swallow
one vodka
after another.
I should have stopped her.

She'd had shots,
tequila
thrown back,

gulped,
her face salty and sticky
and then schnapps, or sours,
who knows
what she downed,
even when I said,
Come on,
Enough –
No.

I gave up
Arguing.
I gave up a fight.
I should have tried harder
To say what I felt,
I was pathetic that night
I know that was my fault."

"Take us back to the crash, Joe,
Just before it happened,
The car?"

"Yeah, I saw it first,
I think, we were going so fast –
and I grabbed at the wheel
but it was so dark.

We turned,
        but we hit it –
                I was just too slow –
I tried to pull us clear,
the car spun off the road."

DO YOU BELIEVE ME?

The men and women of the jury stare –

I'm trying to make the truth bright
set it flaming alight
trying to open their eyes
so that Imogen's story
no longer shines.
I peel back the layers
show them my fear
and why I was scared
why I lied at first,
but now I am here
for the truth to be heard.

CHANGE OF HEART

"Could you please explain to the judge
And the jury, Joe,
Why you changed your plea,
Once you'd already told
The police that it was you
Who was driving the car,
That you were the one
Who'd taken a life?"

My barrister has planned this question –
it's my last chance to explain,
God, help me be clear,
please make this make sense.

MAKING SENSE

"I don't remember saying it,
like the copper said I did.

I only remember Imogen
asking me to take the blame,

to cover for her
when the police asked what had gone on.

And then, when they asked   us,
she lied and said it was   me,
well I didn't want to cause a   fuss,
to cause a massive   scene
right   there
after the   crash
because that poor   woman,"
I draw a   breath,
"Stephanie,   was   dead.
And I wanted to protect   Imogen,
I knew she was   scared.
I felt bad about the   row
about how it had all gone   wrong,
and I thought we'd sort it   out,
that somehow between   us,
we'd get everything   clear,
I never thought she   meant it.
I didn't think I'd end up   here."

CROSS-EXAMINATION

He's almost laughing at me,
the prosecutor who stands
in his long black gown
with his long pale hands
gesturing as if he can bring me down
with a wave of his wand.

Snape, I'd call him, if this was a joke –
and I'm Harry frigging Potter
with more than one scar
fighting to bring the light of truth
out of the dark.

"Mr Goodenough," he begins,
ironic smirk at my name,
"Let's see if we can call a halt
To this tedious game.
Let's see if we can discover
What really happened at last,
Let's see if you'll admit
You were driving too fast,
That you killed a woman
Who'd been working all night,
A nurse,

A mother,
Who devoted her life
to saving other people's lives.

Ladies and gentleman of the jury
If you would be so kind
To refer to the photograph
On page ninety-nine
Of your folders,
The photograph that this young man believes
Is the proof that will help him,
to get out of jail free.

Now let us consider
The likelihood please
That the bruises on his chest
Are, just as he pleads,
A sign of an injury
Sustained that night
Proof that he was not sitting
On the driver's side.

How do we know that the image isn't faked?
How can you be certain that later that day
He didn't go out and inflict this damage
Onto himself,

In a poor attempt to manage
The consequences he faced?

Why didn't he mention it
To the medics, or the police
Who attended the scene
Or even the brief
Who represented Joe,
Who was there by his side
At the station when he was arrested?
I'll tell you why –

Because this is a lie.

What you ought to consider
Is that Joseph already said
That he was guilty of driving
Dangerously,
He already told us
How sorry he is –
And so he should be
Given what he did.

Joseph Goodenough is guilty
I'm sure you agree
Please make sure you remember

Not to let him go free."

I open my mouth to protest
And to tell him to stop,
Twisting the truth,
To stop making things up.

I've been here before,
The silent, sad fool,
I've swallowed back arguments,
Silenced retorts
But I'm not going to do that
I pull him up short.
And I start to speak
Shout over this bloke
Who's so full of hot air
He ought to explode.

"Tell him to stop –
            look, this is bollocks,
                        it's not f-fair
I'm not guilty,
        I wasn't driving.
                    It was Imogen
                            I swear."

WHAT SORT OF MAN ARE YOU?

The prosecutor laughs in my face.

"You're asking this jury to believe
That a big lad like you
Couldn't defend himself
Against a mere girl,
A slip of a thing –
You're saying she forced
You to lie
That you couldn't speak your own mind?

Come on, Mr Goodenough
Do you think this jury's blind?"

SNITCH

Don't tell
Don't rat
Don't act
like the truth is a sacred thing.

But I broke the code,
the unwritten rule
that says
you don't throw your mates to the wolves.

But this isn't school.

There are so many lives to weigh up,
and Stephanie's death
is not a joke.

I'm balancing it all:
Stephanie, me and Mum and Dad –

and on the other side,
the girl
I once
loved.

BROKEN

My dad told me
you have to take responsibility.

But with Imogen
it's like trying to
catch
the wind inside
a net.

Like trying to stop
a star
from exploding.

Like trying to rewind time,
reset a clock
that's already broken.

CONFUSED

Once there was a plan
To face the world together –

We wrote it in the back of her diary
Put our names together inside a heart.

Back then she liked to write with glitter pens,

And I liked the pretty way she wrote my name –
The "O" a heart.

Where did she put that record,
Did she just throw it away?

Because it's evidence, isn't it,
that we meant something,
mean something,
didn't mean to make this mistake.

BELIEVE IT

"Yes," I tell the prosecutor,
"Yes that's right.
Imogen frightened me
into silence and lies."

Even now my voice is shaking
weaker than a little kid's,
but it's still hard to say it
still so hard to have failed.

So hard to say that boys can be hurt
even though they're tall and strong.
That boys can be scared
even when they seem so tough.

Because Imogen lifted my shell
and prodded deep underneath
at flesh unprotected,
she bit with sharp teeth –
she stole chunks of my certainty,
ripped out fistfuls of hope,
she ate up my confidence
and didn't care
that it hurt.

SUMMING UP

My barrister goes for it,
stern and severe
she fixes the jury with a terrible stare.

"What we have here is a good young man
who should never have been part of this sham.

Please do not be fooled by the words of liars –
by anyone who's said that he was the driver.

Another culprit will need to be tried for this crime,
but now it's your duty to put things right.

Joe Goodenough is surely decent and true,
he's done nothing to warrant a guilty verdict from you.

So please, can you in all conscience accept
That he'd do any of the things the prosecution has
    claimed?
The evidence is abundantly clear.
Just one look at that photograph
Should take away any doubt.
There's only one answer
To the question you're asked –
Joe cannot be guilty.
Please do what's right."

WAITING

The jury file out.
How long will it take

354

to decide what to do with my life?

I tried to take back the right
to choose who I'd be,
where I'd go, what I'd become

And it meant standing up
here, and confessing
what I'd done,

Confessing that I was scared and screwed up,
and telling them that just because I look tough, I'm not.

I wonder what they're saying,
what words they will use
when they start to describe
what I did, who I am.

And they have only one choice –
I'm either
Guilty,
Or not.

TIME

There's no sign of the jury and I go to find Mum,
I need to hear her reassure me,
need her calm, her love.

"Oh, Joey," she says,
I'm proud of you, son,
You did ever so well,
my best boy, my love."

How long do we wait?
I watch a fly crawl across a window pane
searching for a crack in the glass,

                                       an escape.

Mum talks to Dad on the phone,
murmuring – she tells him
it went well,
she thinks I'm coming home.

I want to tell her not to raise his hopes.

The suit feels too tight,
I crack my wrists, roll my shoulders
like I've grown bigger,

grown up overnight.

"How long, Mum?" I mutter
when she hangs up
she shrugs, and crosses her fingers.
"Not long I hope."

But it's ages.
Why so long?   Ten minutes,
Then an hour   have passed,
    Time teasing,   and ticking.
        "They're having a laugh."

"Joe, calm down," Mum says,
but I pace the room,
"Can't we go home?
This is a joke."

Then the solicitor's there
barrister too
the look on their faces
tells me it's not good news.

VERDICT

"They're ready for you, Joe."
I hug Mum tight,
in case this is actually goodbye.

I'm expecting the worst –
got to face their decision
by myself.

We rise for the judge
and then it's over to him.
Try not to flinch,
or startle
when he speaks.

"Members of the jury
Do you have a verdict?"

                              "We do."

"Will the defendant please rise."

And time stops again.

Like it did that night

and I see her face –
Stephanie's horrified eyes meet mine.
I wonder what she thought,
if she thought of those she loved
or if she only had her terror
in that moment
before she died.

I look at the jury
and wonder what they see,
if they see her lost life
reflected in me.

I wait for the words
that will decide
what I am.

And I'm not sure I believe
that I'm hearing this right –

"Not guilty,"

the foreman says
and the court stirs, and rumbles,
but I know that I was,
and I always will be

and I fall to my knees,
hear nothing else,
can't speak, can't see –

I can walk away
from this courtroom,
supposedly
free.

LOST

I thought Mum would be waiting,
but it's Annie who's there –
and my smile smashes to the floor
when she grabs me, tells me,
"Joe, oh, I'm sorry – your mum had to go.
Your dad's taken a turn, she's had to go home."

I race out of court and look for a bus,
Annie yelling for me to hold on,
but there's no time
I just run.

Have I ever needed wings more?
Have I ever cursed my slow self?
Now I fail to fly, to find strength,
When it's needed the most.

ABSENCE

Lungs burning
I slam inside our house.

But all is silence.

Empty spaces,
that dip in his chair,
his glasses mended with a twist of tape
lie abandoned on the floor.

Dad, you have left yourself behind in pockets of air
that I fill now with your name, as I holler,
"Where are you, Dad? Where?"

"I'm coming," I shout into my phone
and don't listen as

Mum tries to talk me down
whilst telling me to hurry.

There isn't much time.

RACE

The afternoon sun
is an insult,
its flame
makes me sweat in my suit,
as I weave through traffic
breathing in fumes
fighting to find the fastest route.

When
I stop,
brought up short
by a siren I have to let by,
I let out a shout
to the high blue sky
a gut-wrenching bellow that tears out my insides,
I throw my pain up high to the gods

who don't care, who laugh
and I crash back to earth.

I run on, getting closer
but slower than before
I just need to get there
burn a path to his door –

Dad's waiting
I know it
and once I arrive
I will hold his hand,
I will help him survive.

I'll tell him that he has to cling on,
that he deserves to grow old –
that I will make it easy,
I will carry him,
lift him
high on my shoulders,
I will lead him through darkness
out into the light
I will take him to safety
I will take on his fight.

FINAL WHISTLE

Somehow I find him.
Well,
I find Mum.

And her tears tell me everything –

He's gone.

GOODBYE

I believed
he'd make it,
such misplaced faith.

I chose not to see –
that made it easier for me.

Dad lies still,
his battle for air
over,
the machines sit quiet,
hands folded in a final prayer.

I sit down
and lean my head on his shoulder
and tell him I'm sorry,
I was too late.

ELEGY

No one knows Dad's gone,
no one beyond our little corner of the world –
just me, and Mum,
some friends, my nan
uncles, cousins
aunties, pals, his old school mates,
neighbours.
The church swells up with people and then later the
     pub
is loud
with stories and songs
about a man
who was so strong
that his memory lives on,
in me
his son.

Big man, someone says –
Big Jim, big heart.
And I was always little Joey,
until I grew up.

I raise my glass in a toast to my dad,
and feel his weight on my shoulders,
the ghost of a hand on my back.

GRIEF

Part of me
          the hopeful part
                    the childish heart
Believes that he will
             always
                be
                  just
                     around
the corner.

SHAME

I am very ashamed
of so many things
but mostly
of not understanding
when Imogen said,
"Joe, I'm sad."
I should have done something,
helped her, somehow –
but I let us go bad.

I didn't get it.
I thought she liked
ruining everything.

I tried to make her smile
when she wanted to cry.

And when she hurt me
I didn't realize
she was hurting herself.

It's still hard
to make that make sense
I gave too much of me
to someone else.

VISIT

There is too much left
to say,
but Imogen's gone, charged,
they've put her away.
She's on remand
in a prison miles away.

I write and ask
to see her
and wait for the post,
wait for an answer.

At first she says no,
and then,
suddenly,
it's a yes.

I catch a train and a bus.
I stare at my feet,
and wait –
Imogen walks in,
in her own clothes.
Funny, I thought she'd be wearing
prison scrubs,

I thought she'd be different –
but she looks like herself.

"So why've you come?" she asks,
slouching into the seat.
"What do you want?
Why d'you want to see me?"
She crosses her arms
and her eyes are hard.

I stare at the ceiling,
down at the floor
and then, when she touches me,
I recoil.

I didn't mean to do that.

She flushes red
puts her hands to her cheeks,
and then pushes back her chair
like she's about to get up, and leave.

"I'm sorry," I say, reaching out –
"don't go."

She shakes her head, walks away
then stops at the door,

turns, slowly,
to face me once more.

I stand –
hold her there, for a second,
with my eyes.
There are so many things I need to say –
I want to tell her
I loved her,
but what difference does that make?

I want to say,
It was good, right, Im?
You and me, once.
It wasn't all shit.

I want to say –
I'm sorry it ended like this.

She half smiles,
as if she knows, and says,
"It's all right, Joe – forget it,
I'll be okay."

And then she lifts her bare hand
and walks away.

LOVE

If in the end love is all there is
then I'm not sure what I've been left with.

When I was trapped,
like a bird in a cage
Imogen watched, then flew away.

She fled from me
key held in her teeth
a song on her lips that wasn't the truth.

Trust snapped like a twig
and she would have left me to rot,
my life wrung out –
my future stopped.

But her wings were broken,
she never flew far
and now, walking away,
there's something left of my heart.

FREEDOM

They're waiting,
in Annie's car.
My friends are here, leaning on the horn
summoning me to an adventure.
Summer holidays spool out before us
and we have pockets full of plans,
full of potential.
Annie's driving today,
and we're going far from here,
but I plan to come back
to this place that means home –
I've told Mum I'll stay close.

There are so many
hours
and days
and minutes
left to fill,
so much to taste
and see
and maybe something good in
    the distance,   waiting.

I stare

towards mountains
that I might scale,
stare at a map that we've made, all the seas I could
    sail.

Earthbound,
I know
that my wings have been burnt.
I still find the ashes
on my skin
in my eyes
but I know I can cry myself clean for a while.

I owe it to Dad
To myself,
And my mum
To move carefully forward,
With the truth, and go on.

THE END

ACKNOWLEDGEMENTS

This book has been supported by so many talented and generous people and I have a great deal to be thankful for. Firstly, huge thanks to my wonderful agent Hilary Delamere and also to the wonderful Jessica Hare at The Agency: you're an amazing team.

I am so lucky to be published by Guppy Books. A mega thank you to the awe-inspiring Bella Pearson for her editorial magic, as well as for doing every other thing under the sun. It is such a privilege to work with you and I am so grateful that you go above and beyond. Love and thanks to the wondrous Catherine Alport and Carolyn McGlone; to Amy Dobson, to Hannah Featherstone and to the Michael O'Mara team. A special thank you to Ness Wood for hours spent on the glorious cover. Huge thanks to Colyn for type-setting wizardry and patience!

To my friends who are writers and who have read early drafts and given their unwavering support: Alexia Casale, Lucy Cuthew, Oliver Kent, and the SCBWI NW team. My dear friends, Diana and Juliette, who never fail to encourage me.: thank you. Thank you to amazing Eve Reid for reading and approving.

A MASSIVE thank you to Jenny Downham, Brian Conaghan and Teri Terry for your ridiculously kind words about this book. Thank you for giving up precious time to read and blurb.

To the bloggers and booksellers, reviewers, librarians, teachers and fellow readers and writers IRL and on Twitter. I'm so thankful to be part of such a brilliant YA community.

Thanks to friends and colleagues and all the girls I teach; Team Loreto, all the way! I stole some of the things you sometimes say (obviously not the swearing) – I I RD I'm looking at you. Cheers for the material. And a special thanks to the Grumpy Cats :)

Hugest of thanks to my sisters Margaret and Emily for all your input. You have been outstandingly generous with your time, ideas, words and advice. Thanks also to my mother, Gill, for continuing to put up with me, to Christopher, Felicity and all the fam for being supporters. Love and thanks also to Oliver and Guy and all the Reids.

Final biggest and best thank you to the crucial crew: Alistair, Eve and Scarlett. You're the best. Love you loads.

GUPPY
BOOKS

Guppy Books is an independent children's publisher based in Oxford in the UK, publishing exceptional fiction for children of all ages. Small and responsive, inclusive and communicative, Guppy Books was set up in 2019 and publishes only the very best authors and illustrators from around the world.

From brilliantly funny illustrated tales for five-year-olds to inspiring and thought-provoking novels for young adults, Guppy Books promises to publish something for everyone. If you'd like to know more about our authors and books, go to the Guppy Aquarium on YouTube where you'll find interviews, drawalongs and all sorts of fun.

We hope that our books bring pleasure to young people of all ages, and also to the adults sharing these books with them. Children's literature plays a part in giving both young and old the resources and reflection needed to grow up in today's ever-changing world, and we hope that you enjoy this small piece of magic!

Bella Pearson
Publisher

www.guppybooks.co.uk